OUT OF NOWHERE

GERARD WHELAN was born in Enniscorthy, County Wexford. He has worked in various capacities in several European countries, but now lives in Dublin. His first book, *The Guns of Easter*, won the Bisto Merit Award and the Eilís Dillon Memorial Award. He followed this with *Dream Invader*, which won the Bisto Book of the Year Overall Award in 1998. His third book, a sequel to *The Guns of Easter*, was *A Winter of Spies*, and he has also edited a major anthology of children's literature, *Big Pictures*.

OUT of NOWHERE

An Entertainment

GERARD WHELAN

THE O'BRIEN PRESS
DUBLIN

First published 1999 by The O'Brien Press Ltd,
20 Victoria Road, Dublin 6, Ireland.
Tel. +353 1 4923333; Fax. +353 1 4922777
email: books@obrien.ie
website: www.obrien.ie

ISBN: 0-86278-637-1

British Library Cataloguing-in-publication Data
Whelan, Gerard
Out of nowhere
1.Children's stories
I.Title
823.9'14[J]

1 2 3 4 5 6 7 8 9 10
99 00 01 02 03 04 05 06 07

The O'Brien Press receives
assistance from

The Arts Council
An Chomhairle Ealaíon

Layout and design: The O'Brien Press Ltd.
Colour separations: C&A Print Services Ltd.
Printing: Cox&Wyman Ltd.

Dedicated with respect, admiration
& above all affection
To one of England's more durable exports,
The one and only Ms Carolyn Swift

ACKNOWLEDGEMENTS
Ta very much to the original readers:
Eoin Colfer, Liz Morris, Frank Murphy,
Larry O'Loughlin and Claire Ranson.
Final work on this book was done in New York. It
wouldn't have been possible without David Smith of
Manhattan, who gave me access to his computer,
e-mail and phone.

contents

PART THREE: The Fix-It Men

PART FOUR: These Our Actors

PART ONE: The Weird World

1. The Stone Room

First there was nothing at all. Then a blurred glimpse of robed figures standing over him and a cold feeling of fear. And then again nothing, neither threat nor rest nor dream.

When Stephen came to he was lying on a hard bed. He opened his eyes and found himself looking up at a low ceiling made of plain dark wood. It wasn't a ceiling he recognised, he was certain of that.

He raised his head and looked around. The room he was in looked like a film-set. The walls were of bare stone. Dark curtains were pulled across the window. Such light as leaked through was dim and, beyond the fact that it was daylight, he couldn't guess the time.

Apart from the bed that he lay on, there wasn't much furniture in the room: a large square table, two wooden chairs, a huge cupboard and a small bedside locker. On the table was a large three-branched candlestick with three fat unlit candles standing in it. A large rectangular mirror hung on the wall by the window. The heavy wooden door, the only exit he could see, was closed.

Stephen raised himself on one elbow and looked around slowly. He was sure he'd never seen this place before. It was then, as he tried to remember where he might have expected to wake up, that he became afraid. Because he couldn't remember. He couldn't recall going to bed, and he couldn't recall who he was. Apart from the fact that his name was Stephen, he couldn't remember anything about himself at all.

He lay still, thinking hard. He tried to remember a single other fact about himself, and failed. He was a mystery to himself. Had he been in some kind of accident? But this didn't look like a hospital room. It hardly looked like a room from this century at all.

He was distracted by the sound of a man's voice shouting. The voice shouted again and again. It sounded both pained and angry, but the words were in a language Stephen didn't recognise. There were other voices too now – lower, calmer, soothing. The man stopped shouting, then the other voices stopped too.

Stephen got out of bed, curious, and moved towards the window – the shouting had come from right outside. He saw that he was dressed only in underwear, and looked around for something else to cover himself with. There was a dark robe draped across the foot of the bed. He put it on. As he tied the cord around his waist, the door opened a little. A head peered in. The boy couldn't see the face in the dim light, just a silhouette.

'Ah,' said a thin, accented voice. 'You are awake, young man.'

'Yes,' Stephen said, not knowing what else to say.

The head nodded. 'Good. I'll tell the abbot.'

The head withdrew, and the door closed. The boy stood staring at it. The abbot? Was this place an abbey? Then, remembering what he'd meant to do, he crossed to the window and pulled back the curtain. Bright light burst in, almost frightening him. He was looking down from an upstairs window. Opposite the window he saw cloisters, a stone wall pierced by arched windows, and an open doorway with shadow beyond. Below him lay a courtyard filled with light. In the middle of the area he could see stood an old-fashioned covered well. There were no people in sight.

From the corner of his eye Stephen caught a glimpse of movement within the room. He turned quickly and faced himself in the mirror. He stared at a stranger. Dark hair, pale face, a slight form. Worried eyes. Thirteen years old? Fourteen? He had no idea.

He was afraid.

There was a knock at the door and two men came in. Both wore long dark robes. One was talking as they came in, and Stephen recognised the voice of his recent visitor. He was a thin, slight, balding old man with a shrewd face that looked lived-in. But it was his companion who held Stephen's attention.

This man seemed to glide into the room. He was very tall and very thin. His hair, partly covered by a skullcap, was salt-and-pepper grey and cropped tight. His head was large, his face long and angular. His lips were thin. He had deep-set, watchful brown eyes; at the moment they were watching Stephen, frankly, carefully.

The man glided to the table and stood there without speaking. The other man stopped walking too, but kept talking.

'… we're doing our best,' he was saying, 'but there simply aren't enough of us. We can't watch all of them all of the time. Philip only turned his back for a moment. He's very annoyed with himself.'

The tall man raised one hand. The shorter man stopped speaking abruptly, as if he'd been switched off. The tall man – monk, rather, for they were obviously monks – didn't take his eyes off Stephen as he spoke to his companion. His English was perfect, but to Stephen his accent sounded foreign.

'Philip is always annoyed with himself,' he said quietly. 'Tell him to calm down. He won't listen, but tell him anyway.'

The small monk nodded and left. The other stood looking at Stephen. Stephen remembered what the first monk had said when he found him awake. This, then, must be the abbot. Stephen had a hundred questions he wanted to ask, but he didn't know where to begin. The abbot's brown eyes seemed to bore into his, to look right past them and inside his head.

At last the abbot spoke.

'You're sane,' he said. It wasn't a question. He sounded relieved.

The boy stared at him.

'Am I?' he asked.

The abbot looked concerned.

'Are you in pain?'

'No. But I'm scared. What happened to me?'

The monk made a fluid gesture with his long hand, indicating a chair.

'Please,' he said, 'sit down.'

Stephen realised that his knees were trembling. He felt weak. He sat. The abbot sat opposite him.

'I'll tell you what I can,' the monk said. 'But first I must ask you one question: can you remember anything at all about what happened to you?'

'No. I was hoping you could tell me. My name is Stephen, I know that. But I don't know a single other thing about myself. I don't know who I am.'

He heard a ghost of panic in his final sentence. But the abbot breathed what sounded like a sigh of relief.

'Thank heaven,' he said.

Stephen couldn't believe his ears. His fear and frustration turned to anger.

'I've lost my memory,' he said, 'and all you can say is "Thank heaven"?'

'I beg your pardon,' the monk said. 'I forget my manners. It's just that I'm so used to talking about this now. We speak of little else. And so few of our guests are as lucky as you.'

His words made no sense to Stephen. 'What happened to me?' he demanded.

'I don't know,' the abbot replied.

'But you still call me lucky?'

The monk rested his chin in one hand. He pursed his lips and cast his brown eyes downwards. Without their penetrating gaze, his face looked different. It was still strong, but you could see a strained tiredness there too.

'I'm trying to put myself in your position,' he said slowly. 'So as to know how best to explain it to you. We know so little ourselves, really.'

Stephen wanted to scream at him to stop dawdling. But then the brown eyes flicked upwards again and held his in a steady gaze. They weren't the kind of eyes you screamed at.

'You're not the only person we're caring for,' the monk said. 'There are five others – so far. The first strayed in on Sunday night. A poor, lone unfortunate, we thought, a dazed accident victim, perhaps – though there's very little traffic hereabouts, even in the tourist season. He arrived in the middle of the night. We were all long asleep, but he made so much noise he woke us. It was too late that night to do anything about it, so we sedated him and put him to bed, meaning to contact the police on Monday morning to explain the situation. Well, he was certainly a poor unfortunate: but he wasn't alone. We found you wandering near the abbey on Tuesday, also dazed and disoriented. You were the third person we found. Today is Thursday, and we have six.'

Stephen was stunned.

'In four days?' he asked. 'You've found six people with amnesia in four days?'

'I wish we had. Including yourself, we've found only two amnesiacs.'

'And the others?'

'Ah,' said the abbot. 'The others.' He was silent.

'You still haven't contacted the police?' Stephen burst out.

'Or a hospital?'

'That's the problem, do you see,' the abbot said. 'There don't seem to be any police or hospitals.'

'What?' Stephen gasped.

'Something …' the monk began, hesitantly, '… something has happened.'

'What do you mean?'

The monk sighed again. 'I don't know,' he said. 'That's the simple truth. But I suspect it must be something very terrible. Apart from those of you who've wandered in, we can't contact anyone. We can't even find anyone. Any houses we've searched are empty. So is the closest village. We can't contact anyone on the telephone. All the animals are still there – but not a single human being.'

Stephen couldn't take this in. It sounded foolish. 'Radio?' he said. 'Television?'

The abbot shook his head. 'We have both,' he said. 'On Sunday night everything was as usual, but since Monday morning there's been nothing on any channel, local, national or foreign. And even to try them we have to use our own small generator because there's no electricity either.'

Stephen was stunned. An awful thought came to him. He had a terrible vision of mushroom clouds.

'A war?' he croaked.

But the abbot shook his head. 'We'd have seen something,' he said. 'And so far as I know, there are no weapons which can destroy humans and leave animals alive. Not yet, anyway, though I'm sure someone's working on it. No. All we know is that on Sunday everything was normal, but by Monday morning everything had changed. Something – whatever it was – happened during the night.'

A sudden thought struck the boy. 'What about the other four people who don't have amnesia? Don't they remember anything?'

The monk sighed again. It was a lonely sound. 'Oh, yes,' he said, with immense sadness. 'They remember things all right. Two of them remember the end of the world. One even remembers creating it. They remember monsters and spaceships and vampires. One recalls living in fairyland. Another one says nothing at all – except sometimes he howls.'

He shook his head sadly. 'The reason I was pleased that you'd lost your memory,' he said, 'can be explained by the very first words I said to you when I came in. Do you remember what they were?'

Stephen didn't have to think. 'Yes. You said: "You're sane".'

'Indeed. You're sane. So is our other amnesia victim. But those of our guests who seem to have memories, they, alas, are not sane. None of them. They are all hopelessly mad.'

2. The Blond Girl

Whether from the abbot's news or from his own weakness, Stephen suddenly felt faint. He almost collapsed, and the monk had to help him back to his bed.

'The best thing you can do now,' the monk said, 'is to get some rest.'

'You don't really think I'll sleep after what you've told me, do you?'

'Then the next best thing would be some proper food. You must be hungry.'

At the mention of food the boy's stomach rumbled. The abbot smiled.

'No need to say more,' he said. 'I'm busy now, but I'll come back to see you later. I'm afraid we're all kept very busy just coping with our other patients. Our numbers are very low at the moment – only three Brothers and a novice.'

'This is really an abbey? You're real monks? I don't mean to be rude, it just seems … strange.'

'Ours is a lay order,' the abbot said. 'So I suppose, in a way, we're not "real" monks. In a way you could even say that it's not a "real" abbey. We train novices here, so we're really no more than a glorified school. Now, I'll stop talking and send you up some food. You must be starving – I'll ask Fräulein Herzenweg to bring something to you.'

'You have women working here?'

'Oh no, not normally. It's hardly the done thing in a monastery. She's our other amnesia case – Fräulein Kirsten Herzenweg, your fellow patient.'

'But you know her whole name.'

'She had letters addressed to a person of that name. It may not be her name at all – she doesn't recognise it – but it's nice to have even a tentative identification. I'm sure you understand.'

'Oh yes,' said Stephen wistfully. 'Yes, I do.'

'Stephen' was only a word. He felt sure that it was his name, but how could he be certain? It was only half a name, anyway. He envied Fräulein Herzenweg that tiny luxury of an extra word.

'I suppose I had no papers?' he asked.

'No. No papers of any kind. I'm sorry.'

'You've no need to apologise,' Stephen said. 'It sounds as though you saved my life, and I haven't even thanked you.'

The abbot smiled.

'No disrespect,' he said, 'but we'd have done as much for anyone. You rest now, and eat, and get some strength back. Then you can help us to deal with whatever this is. That will be all the thanks we need.'

He left the room with his long, gliding step, closing the wooden door behind him. Stephen lay on his bed, trying not to think about himself, whoever he might be. Instead he thought about Fräulein Herzenweg, his 'fellow patient'. Maybe her lot wasn't so enviable after all. She must wonder if Fräulein Herzenweg was a stranger whose coat or bag she'd picked up in passing. Maybe the real Fräulein Herzenweg was dead, or maybe she was one of the other patients – one of the mad ones. And what was a name worth on its own, anyway? It was only a couple of words – it didn't make up a whole person.

He was so busy thinking about Fräulein Herzenweg's name that he gave no thought to the person attached to it. If he had any image at all, he pictured a German woman in her thirties or forties. A timid tap on the door interrupted his thoughts and a small, long-faced young girl with short, very blond hair came into the room carrying a tray. She looked about his own age, which seemed almost stupid to think since he didn't know what that was.

'Hello,' she said, grinning at him.

'Fräulein Herzenweg?'

'Yes,' she said. 'Kirsten Herzenweg,' and there was a touch of pride in the declaration.

'You're German?'

'Actually, I seem to be Danish. Three of the monks here are from the continent and have quite a number of languages between them, so we checked. I speak okay French, good German and fluent English, but my native language seems to be Danish. Just think, I can remember all those languages but I can't remember anything about my own *life*? Isn't it crazy?'

She was carrying a cloth-covered tray. Now she sort of brandished it at him.

'Look,' she said. 'Food!'

Stephen's stomach rumbled again. It seemed to be fretting that its owner might not speak up for it. Kirsten Herzenweg laughed at the sound – a curiously carefree laugh for someone in her situation.

'Now,' she said, 'I've eaten already, but I'll have tea with you if I may.'

'Please,' Stephen said, trying to show some manners. His mind, like his eyes, fixed on the tray as the girl put it on the big table and whisked the cloth away. Then he went and sat, and for the next ten minutes he ate ravenously. Kirsten said he'd eaten nothing since his arrival, except some broth that the monks had managed to pour down his throat. That explained the abbot's reference to 'proper' food.

Kirsten poured strong tea into plain, brown mugs.

'There's coffee here too,' she said, 'but very little. It's a real treat. We've just about run out of a lot of things. The monks weren't prepared for anything like this. We plan a foraging expedition to one of the towns tomorrow.'

He heard pride in her voice when she used the word 'we'.

'Is there really no clue as to what happened?' he asked.

'No. There's no news of any kind. Not a soul to be found so far except those poor people – *we* poor people, I should say.' She gave a little shudder. 'It's terrible to think what might have become of us if the monks hadn't found us, isn't it?'

'I suppose so,' Stephen said. Personally, he found what had happened to them pretty terrible anyway, whatever it had been. 'But there must be something out there. Have the monks searched?'

'Only as far as the nearest village, and that's just a cluster of houses at a crossroads. They've been up to their eyes looking after all of us. But tomorrow, Philip and I are going to the local market town. It's the main town in the area. Maybe we'll find people there.'

'Maybe you'll even find people who are, you know, all right. The inhabitants.'

Kirsten made a face.

'I doubt it,' she said. 'It's only about twenty kilometres away. If there were any people there, surely they'd have come looking for us by now. No. The trip tomorrow will be a major expedition, but I don't think anyone expects to find people in the town, much as we'd love to.'

'But they have to find people soon, I mean, *everybody* can't have just disappeared into thin air! It's not possible!'

'There's nothing on radio or television,' she reminded him. 'No electricity …'

'There must be a simple explanation. Maybe it's just a local thing. How could such a big disaster happen so suddenly? Even if everyone was dead, there'd be bodies. It's just impossible!'

'But it's happened,' she said gently. 'Local or not, it's happened.'

They talked about the situation for a while. It saved them from talking about themselves, which is a hard thing to do when you don't know who you are. After he'd called the girl Fräulein Herzenweg a few times, she stopped him.

'Please,' she said. 'You sound like the monks! Call me Kirsten.'

'You think that's really your name?'

She'd obviously thought about this.

'It's strange,' she admitted. 'I mean, Kirsten is a good, solid Danish name, but Herzenweg is German. Maybe my family came from Germany originally. The letters in my pocket were both addressed to *Fräulein* Kirsten Herzenweg – that's a German form of address. Oh well, in a way I rather *like* being a mystery. It makes me feel important.'

'And the letters themselves?' Stephen asked. 'Did they have any useful information?'

'No,' she said wistfully. 'There were three envelopes. One was a bank statement showing a money transfer, and the other two were empty.'

'What about postmarks? Where were they all sent from?'

'The empty envelopes were posted from Belgium. The bank statement was from Dublin.'

'Dublin?'

She gave him a puzzled look.

'My God!' she said. 'You don't even know what country we're in, do you?'

Stephen thought for a moment.

'Ireland,' he said finally, not knowing how he knew, but still certain that he was right.

Kirsten nodded and smiled.

'Yes,' she said. 'Your home country, to judge by your accent. Maybe I'm a tourist.'

'Did the other … 'patients' have anything to identify them?'

'No. None of them. Only me.'

Again her voice was proud, as though she'd been somehow responsible for this.

Stephen soon felt tired. He hadn't recovered from his weakness, and the food was making him sleepy. Kirsten noticed.

'Rest,' she said. 'You'll feel much better in the morning. At least, that's how it was with me.'

She left, taking the tray with her. Stephen got into bed and lay awake for a few minutes afterwards, thinking about her. He didn't know what to make of Kirsten Herzenweg. She didn't seem very disturbed by her amnesia. She was, she'd said, concentrating on the present. Maybe he could learn from her example.

'The past is gone anyway,' she'd said. 'Maybe I'd hate it if I knew about it. Maybe I was someone awful, or worse, maybe I was someone boring! Perhaps I'll never find out who I was. But in the meantime the present is here, and I'm here, and I'm needed. The monks need all the help they can get right now.'

It seemed sensible enough. In the middle of thinking so, Stephen fell asleep.

3. The Bearded Monk

Stephen was woken at some dead hour of the night by a dreadful sound – a long, singing howl that made his flesh creep and the hairs on the back of his neck stand erect. He was terrified for a moment, not knowing where he was. Just as he started to think that he'd dreamed it, he heard it again. It was the sound a lonely, wounded night would make, if lonely, wounded nights could make sounds. It also sounded like it came from just below his window.

Stephen was shivering in a cold sweat. He wanted to crawl under the quilt and pull it over his head. Instead, he made himself get out of bed, go to the window and look out. The window was ajar, and the sweet air of the summer night brought in a scent of distant greenery. The dark blue sky was spangled with shimmering stars. The moon was fat and silver, and it lit the courtyard clearly with a cold, white light.

In the middle of the courtyard, a very tall man was moving in crazy circles around the well. He was being chased by a young monk who seemed in no great hurry to catch him. He trailed half-heartedly in the tall man's ragged course, not even trying to catch up with him. The fugitive himself didn't seem to notice the monk.

'Where are you?' he roared out suddenly to someone or something. 'Unshade me! It *hurts*!'

'*Unshade me*?' thought Stephen, puzzled. But he was sure that was what he had said. The man was old – a big old stick of a man with a gaunt face and raggy white hair that shone silver in the moonlight. His head was thrown back as he staggered around, howling at the moon. Stephen shuddered at the weird sight.

The grotesque pair rounded the well a few times. Then another monk entered the courtyard from a doorway somewhere beneath Stephen's window, a big, bearded man who stood for a moment, watching the chase. Then he snapped at the young monk in a stern voice with an Irish accent – the first Stephen had heard.

'Catch up, you little eejit! You're like a pup after an ould buck rabbit, half afraid to catch what it's hunting.'

Spurred on by this, or perhaps more afraid of the newcomer than of the old man, the pursuer put on a spurt of speed. He caught up with the staggering figure easily, and threw his arms around his waist. The fugitive lashed out with one thin arm and sent him sprawling. But the monk was suddenly game – he threw himself bodily at the man, grabbing hold of him again. This time the old man just kept going, dragging the monk behind him. It would have looked funny if it hadn't been so sinister.

'He's too strong!' the monk shouted in a panicky voice.

The bearded monk gave a loud sigh. He went over and stood in the old man's path. Stephen noticed that he was almost as tall as the old man, and heavily built.

'Such gods as there be, please forgive me,' the big monk said. Then he punched the old man, once, in the jaw. The fugitive grunted and went down like a pole-axed cow, pulling the young monk down with him. With a little squawk, the monk scrambled to his feet. He stood looking from one big man to the other.

'You *hit* him!' he said, sounding outraged and impressed all at once.

The big monk sighed.

'I did,' he said. 'I hit him.' He put a hand on the young monk's shoulder. 'It's never nice, son,' he said. 'But sometimes it does just simplify things. He'll be grand when he wakes up.'

'But won't it hurt him afterwards?'

The big monk bent down and heaved the long form of the old man over his shoulder. He straightened up again.

'There's something so big hurting this one,' he said, 'that a puck in the jaw won't make much difference.'

He set off across the courtyard lightly carrying the old man across his shoulder, draped like a rolled-up rug. The young monk followed.

After they'd gone, Stephen stayed for a long time looking out at the empty night. His skin crawled, and he pitied himself. What had happened in the world? Who were these unfortunate people? And who, for that matter, was he?

4. Breakfast

The next morning Kirsten woke him early, bringing breakfast on a tray. She seemed almost giddy at the prospect of the morning's expedition, which she insisted on calling 'The Raid'. Stephen laughed at her.

'It's only natural that I'm excited,' she said, not minding his amusement. 'I am Danish after all, my ancestors were Vikings. Raiding must be in my blood!'

It was impossible not to smile at her enthusiasm, but Stephen wondered how she managed it in the circumstances.

Kirsten sat by the table as he ate his breakfast, but she was so excited she couldn't sit still. Stephen hadn't known that it was possible to hop from foot to foot while sitting down, but she proved that it was. She talked non-stop, fantasising about what they might find on the expedition. She really didn't seem upset by the whole situation. If anything, the mystery seemed to excite her all the more.

'You're coming with us, aren't you?' she asked. 'If you feel up to it, I mean.'

Stephen wasn't sure how he felt, but he knew that he couldn't pass up the chance to see this brave new world. He was unnerved by the situation, but he was very curious too.

'You're definitely going?' he asked.

'Of course! I wouldn't miss it for anything. This is like living in a movie!'

But what kind of movie? he wondered. He remembered last night's howling. It had made him feel like he was in a horror film, and horror films tended to have monsters in them.

'It's not a movie,' he reminded her. 'It's real. We're not on some adventure holiday.'

'Our expedition today is important,' Kirsten replied. 'There's very little food left in the abbey. The monks get most of their food from their farm, but they don't have enough supplies stored to deal with six extra mouths. And there are replacement parts and fuel needed for the generator, and clothes for me – I can hardly ask Philip to pick underwear for me, can I? I do know how serious the situation is – or may be. But, at the same time, there's no way I'm going to miss this raiding party, I mean, it even sounds funny, doesn't it: the monastery raiding party?'

He had to admit that, yes, it did sound funny.

'The abbot insists on calling it a "reconnaissance",' Kirsten continued. 'But Philip just laughs when he hears that and says, "Paul, I always knew you were a Jesuit at heart". Which Paul doesn't like, because he's not even a Christian. And then again he's Swiss – very serious!'

'What do you mean, he's *not* a Christian? He's a *monk*!'

'Yes, but this isn't a Christian order. I'll tell you about it later!'

'But–'

But Kirsten had sat still as long as her excitement would allow, and was already at the door.

'I have to help Philip finalise the list of supplies,' she said over Stephen's protests. 'We call it "the shoplifting list". Philip won't admit it, but he's just as excited as I am. He's dying to see what's *out there*. I think he's secretly enjoying all of this. Come and join us in the kitchen when you're dressed.'

'Maybe Philip's ancestors were Vikings, too,' Stephen said.

Her laughter hung in the air after the door closed behind her.

Stephen finished breakfast quickly and went to the cupboard. His clothes were unfamiliar to him. They were perfectly ordinary: tee shirt and sweatshirt, dark denim jeans, socks and trainers. Everything, including the shoes, was spotlessly clean. He presumed they'd been laundered since his arrival. Although he knew that the monks would already have checked, he still went through the pockets carefully. There was nothing in any of them. He hadn't really expected to find anything, but he was disappointed anyway.

'You're stupid,' he said to himself. He suddenly felt that he was standing on a very thin surface, and that under the surface there was a great, sucking depth of something thick and black and smothering. He dressed quickly, trying hard to think of nothing except the journey ahead and what they might find.

5. Fresh Air

Stephen walked down the stone corridor outside his room. At its end was a stairway. His soft soles made no sound on the stone steps. At the bottom of the stairs he startled a young monk who was on his knees, scrubbing flagstones in the hallway. The monk jerked back in surprise, nearly knocking over the bucket of sudsy water that stood beside him. Stephen recognised him as the young monk from the courtyard the night before. The big, bearded man must have been Brother Philip – he'd suspected as much.

'I'm sorry,' Stephen said. 'I didn't mean to startle you.'

The young monk's face reddened. 'You … you're the guest from upstairs,' he stammered.

'Yes,' Stephen said. 'I am.' He repeated his apology.

'It's nothing,' the monk said. 'Really. It's just that I didn't hear you coming, and when I saw you standing over me …' His voice trailed off, embarrassed, and he made a vague gesture with the wire-bristled scrubbing-brush in his hand. 'I thought you might be one of the confined ones. They get out sometimes, no matter how closely we watch them. Some of them are very strong and … crazy.'

Stephen realised that the young monk was very afraid. He

could think of nothing reassuring to say, so instead he asked for directions to the kitchen. The monk indicated an open, arched doorway beside them that led outside.

'Right across the courtyard,' he said, pointing with the scrubbing-brush. 'Go through the door directly opposite. That's the kitchen wing. I don't know whether Brother Philip and Fräulein Herzenweg are in the kitchens or the storeroom, but both rooms are right through there.'

The courtyard was neither as small nor as bare as it had looked from his upstairs window. Looking around and up, Stephen saw that his own room was in one of the two longer arms of a building that was shaped like a square-cornered U. The kitchen was in the opposite arm. To his left, forming the shorter base of the U, stood the main building of the monastery. It was built around a bell-tower that rose above two great wooden doors, which were standing open. On the fourth side, to his right, the top of the U was closed off by a high stone wall, pierced by a large gateway. The wooden gates, which were even bigger than the doors in the bell-tower, were also open.

The courtyard itself was partly flagged, partly gravelled. The well stood in the centre. In front of the main building was a strip of lawn, and between the lawn and the wall of the building itself lay a flowerbed riotous with colour. A flagstone path leading to the great doors bisected both flowerbed and lawn.

It was a very pleasant place in the morning sun. Overhead the sky was a brilliant, cloudless blue. The air was fresh and sweet, heavy with the scent of flowers and the humming of bees. A summer world. It seemed far too beautiful a world to have spawned a great disaster.

He walked carefully across the stone flags – after several days in bed, his legs felt unsteady. The fresh air alone made him dizzy. His head swam with a riot of sensations – the bright light and the heat, the colours and the buzzing of bees, the scents of flowers. The world seemed completely strange to him, as though he'd spent years locked up in an airless cell. And still the questions chased each other round and round in his mind, as they'd done since he'd first woken the day before: who was he? what had happened? where was everyone else?

It was all too much. Stephen felt light-headed and a weak surge of panic welled up in him. He stopped by the well, leaning on its old stone parapet, breathing in the cool, damp air that drifted up from its depths. The bucket, hung from a long rope coiled around a wooden winch, had been recently used – maybe by the monk who was scrubbing the floor. Fat drops of water were dripping from its base. It took a while for each drop to plink into the water below. It was deep water that would be cool on the hottest day.

Stephen leaned over the well, looking in. Far below he saw the surface of the water, a little circle of reflected blue marred by the dark reflection of his own head. As he looked, the reflection of another head appeared beside his own, a very blond-haired head. He felt the physical warmth of someone standing right beside him, brushing against him. It was

Kirsten. He hadn't heard her coming. He looked up, smiling. Then he stopped. The smile froze on his face. There was nobody there. He looked around frantically, but he was alone in the courtyard. He was sweating again. He shivered in the heat.

6. The Shoplifting List

Inside the kitchen wing it was cool. When he walked through the doorway, Stephen found himself in another stone room with more wooden furniture. It looked like a storeroom. The walls, from floor to ceiling, were covered with cupboards and shelves of various sizes. The centre of the floor was taken up by an enormous table with rank after rank of large, closed drawers from table top down to the ground. To either side of him were two doorless arches leading to other unseen rooms beyond.

He heard Kirsten's voice off to his left and went that way. He paused before entering the room. The incident in the courtyard had shaken him badly. Perhaps he was going mad too. But he simply refused to think about it. He would put it down to weakness and confusion, to the shocks that his system had certainly had. What he had to do now was to appear as normal as possible, otherwise they mightn't let him go along, and he felt he simply had to see this empty world. He couldn't really believe in it until he did.

'Fresh fruit,' Kirsten was saying as he walked into the room. She was standing beside the big, bearded monk he'd seen in the courtyard the night before. He'd been right, this was Brother Philip.

The room was very like the first one he had come through, but here there was an enormous, old-fashioned cooking range and shelves of pans and utensils. Kirsten and the monk were concentrating on a notebook she was holding, both of them looking hard at it as Kirsten checked off items with a pen. Stephen was quite close before either of them noticed him. It was the big monk who looked up first. For a moment he frowned, and it was an ugly look, as though he resented anyone coming so near without his noticing. Then it passed, and his face was pleasant again. Kirsten looked up and smiled.

'Hello,' she said brightly. 'Philip, have you met Stephen?'

'Ah yes,' he said. 'Our new helper. Hello, young fellow. I'm Brother Philip – the monastery's token Irishman.'

Stephen shook the monk's extended hand. It was a hard hand, strong and capable.

'I'm Stephen,' he said. He felt he sounded too sure. Was that really his name? It sounded stupid when he said it out loud.

The monk seemed to read his mind. 'You know,' he said, 'names aren't cut in stone. All of us here – we monks – chose new names when we came to the monastery. Sometimes it's good to get away from what you were before.'

'That's what I told him,' Kirsten said. 'Maybe he was a thief before! Or a murderer!'

Philip smiled down at them through his beard. He pretended to examine the boy, who was maybe half a metre shorter than him.

'Aye,' he said, 'he's a dangerous-looking type all right.'

He took the notebook from Kirsten.

'You're coming on this raid of ours?' he asked Stephen.

'If that's all right.'

Philip nodded. 'It's good.' He smiled. 'Maybe you can calm this young one down. We'd need a moving-van to bring half the stuff she wants to thieve, and a gang of brickies to shift it.'

Kirsten giggled.

'Maybe it's the only chance I'll ever have to be a major criminal,' she said.

'You obviously don't know our local market town,' said Philip laughing.

He looked at his watch.

'I want to talk to the abbot before we go,' he said. 'Why don't you two have a last look at the list? Maybe Stephen can think of something we forgot.'

He laughed again as he went out the door.

When Stephen read the list he understood Philip's laughter. There were about ten pages of items, many of them highly unlikely. The notion that he might add anything to it was ludicrous.

'This looks like you're getting ready for a siege!' he said.

Kirsten put on a playfully mysterious face.

'Ah,' she said. 'But who knows what will happen next? We have to be ready for any eventuality!'

'Well,' he said, 'I think this lot will equip you for anything short of a flood. And that seems hardly likely in the mountains.'

Kirsten's excitement was funny to see. Watching her, Stephen felt an odd feeling of fondness. The prospect of an empty world seemed to excite her strangely. Stephen, on the other hand, couldn't think of it without wondering what had happened to all the people. Many things might have happened to them, and a lot of those things were bad. Still, it seemed a shame to ruin Kirsten's excitement by reminding her of that.

When Philip came back he was brisk and businesslike, but under his calm exterior Stephen thought he detected an excitement that almost matched Kirsten's. It was a different kind of excitement though, a peculiar mixture of glee and unease which Stephen felt he must be imagining. They chatted briefly, but still Stephen sensed the same mixed feelings under Philip's calm, amused exterior.

So what's the problem if he's mixed up? Stephen asked himself. It's exactly how you feel yourself.

But Philip made him uneasy in a way that was even odder than the fondness he'd felt for Kirsten. He chided himself. They were both total strangers. What did he know about either of them?

'Right,' the big monk said finally. 'That's everything, I think. You're sure you're up to this, Kirsten?'

Kirsten gave him a withering look.

'Just you try to leave me behind,' she said. 'I'd follow on foot.'

'I declare to God,' Philip said, 'but I believe you would.'

He picked up the notebook, closed the cover and slapped the table with it.

'Very well, lady and gentleman,' he said. 'There's a world out there waiting to be pillaged, a rotten job, I know, but someone has to do it! Let's go.'

And he led the way out with yet another laugh, which to Stephen sounded oddly forced. It was the last laugh that Philip would have for quite some time.

7. Agents In The Flesh

Sense came slowly. I didn't hurry it. It was like waking from a special kind of sleep. I was just an awareness, receiving information through limited but vivid senses. I was in a body.

I knew where I was, more or less. To be in a *place* ... the mere thought of it sent a shiver of excitement up the spine. A light sweat broke out on the skin, and I squirmed with a rich mix of fear, joy and tension. This is like no other feeling. Once felt, it can't be mistaken for anything else.

I opened the eyes. There was a blue sky overhead. Blueness. I was out in the open, under a blue sky. I lay still for another moment, savouring the old sensations. I could feel the eyes blinking, reacting to the myriad colours and shapes. I could feel the muscles in the eyelids, perfect, tiny. I had a throat. I swallowed, to feel the movement there. I felt the mouth smile.

I sat up. I was on green grass in a clearing on a wooded slope. A hillside. I turned the head (my head, I reminded myself, for the moment at least), and looked around. I could see no sign of my friend.

A small brown animal crouched in the long grass, watching me. It stood, bright-eyed and trembling, wrinkling its whiskered snout, obviously confused. I looked like a human, yet it couldn't sense danger.

'Come,' I said. The small thing hesitated, then came shyly over.

'Hello there, creature,' I said. The animal grew more confident as it got closer. It sensed my lack of humanness. It sniffed at my foot. I felt my smile widen. It was so simple, sitting here on a hillside, under a blue sky, with another animal. This was the miracle we'd forsaken.

There was a loud, rustling crash from the edge of the clearing, as though a much larger animal was floundering in the undergrowth there. That would be my friend. I rose carefully to the feet, *my* feet. The little brown animal froze, trying to decide whether or not the new sound was threatening.

'Not to you, little one,' I told it softly. 'We're no threat to you.'

I went towards the sounds. They were coming from a depression in the ground, a deep hollow filled almost to its brim with undergrowth and high drifts of old, dead leaves. A loud rustling came from somewhere among the foliage, followed by a string of curses. As I stood on the lip of the hollow I saw my friend's arm and hand thrust up suddenly out of the leaf-drift. His head followed and he looked up at me with a sour expression.

'I bet,' he said, 'this is somebody's idea of a joke.'

His other hand appeared, clutching a grey hat. He looked funny, standing there. I had to laugh. It felt good.

'They wanted to give you a soft landing,' I said.

He waded through the banks of leaves and scrambled up

the side of the hollow. His dark suit was stained with leaf mould and dotted with fragments of broken twigs and leaves. He brushed it down with an air of injured dignity. They'd given me a fairly natty outfit too, I noticed, a tailored two-piece in charcoal grey with a fine black stripe. We looked terribly respectable – it was a pity there'd be nobody to see us. At least, nobody who'd appreciate the effect – nobody who'd live long after meeting us.

'I see you've made contact with a native already,' my friend said. I followed his gaze. The little brown animal stood shyly nearby, watching us. It had raised itself up on its hind legs and was sniffing our scents, puzzled.

'Go home, thing,' I told it. 'We're trouble.'

'That we are,' my friend said amiably. 'Death on legs, that's us. Blood smoking in the dust and mothers crying. Feeding of ravens and shields with broken bosses.'

'Oh shut up,' I said. 'You'll frighten it. Anyway, they don't use shields here anymore. You're old-fashioned, you are. A fellow has to keep up with the times.'

My friend finished brushing himself off. He put his hand on his head, straightened his tie, put his hands on his hips and stood looking around him appreciatively.

'Marvellous!' he said. 'The old place looks good no matter what they do to it.'

He spat on the ground, and then leaned down and looked at the spit. He laughed.

'You know,' he said, 'I should come back more often. I'd almost forgotten what it was like.'

'Spitting?'

'No, Dolt! *Being*.'

I looked around at the trees.

'Well,' I said. 'Here we are. This is called a hill, right?'

'Yes. We can go over it, or around it, or just down.'

I thought about that.

'Over, around or down,' I said slowly. 'Yes, it's all coming back to me now. We'll go up. When you're up you can see further.'

We set off uphill at a gentle pace. The trees thinned and then yielded to a barer landscape of thin soil and naked rock. My friend murmured with pleasure when we passed a bank of yellow-blossomed furze bushes.

'Wonderful!' he said. 'I do love *places*.'

It wasn't a hill we were on, but a mountain. At length we reached its bare rock summit. From there we could assess our surroundings. Around us were other slopes. The sun was bright, the sky nearly cloudless. We stood on the mountain and took in the view.

'We'll keep going this way,' my friend said, pointing. 'The sea's behind us. There should be some class of a road over that way.'

We set off in silence, watchful. The world is always a dangerous place, and here we were inside the exclusion zone itself – anyone we met would be either confused or an enemy.

We were skirting the lower slopes of our third or fourth mountain when I sensed the pain. It hung in the still air like smoke. My friend felt it at the same time. We looked around.

'Over there,' my friend said.

I looked and saw a patch of colour on the hillside. A middle-aged man. He was dead, killed recently and messily — the body was still warm. His killer, or killers, couldn't be far away.

'Time to go to work,' said my friend quietly. His face had lost its smile and taken on a prim, purse-lipped look of disapproval. I knew that look from other faces he'd worn when we were in the strange thing called Time. Reaching into his pocket, he took out the little case. He opened it and took out the crystals, handing one of them to me. The water-rounded pebbles, shot through with quartz, felt hard in my soft hand. My friend put the case back into his pocket. I licked my lips. It was always hard to adjust in the beginning, and I hadn't been on a job like this for two thousand years. Nobody had, really.

My friend looked at the carcass with disdain.

'They're acting like humans,' he said.

It was an extreme insult, but I understood how he felt. Our kind has always hated waste.

We went ahead, warily, but we didn't need to look far for the killer. He wasn't even attempting to hide. He was standing on top of a big rock, a boulder deposited by some glacier long ago, even before *our* time. He was a young boy, maybe fifteen or sixteen years old. The stench of his madness got stronger as we drew near. He stood there looking down at us arrogantly as we approached. His eyes were wild, and he was covered with dirt. In one hand he carried a long, curved knife such as men used to cut crops — a sickle. I found it hard to take my eyes off the blade.

The boy made no move either to run or to attack.

'He's on his own,' my friend said softly. 'He really is crazy, just standing there like that. Do you want to ask him anything first?'

'What's the point? Unshade him.'

Still the death-drunk boy made no move, although he must have known who we were. By now he must at least have felt the presence of the crystals. About five metres from the rock my friend stopped. He raised his arm and pointed the crystal at the boy. Now, finally, the boy did move, but it was too late. It had been too late from the moment we arrived.

The crystal's power hit the boy square in the body and threw him back off the rock. When we walked around it we found him lying on the grass. He wasn't breathing. The open dead eyes still held hate.

'That's one down anyway,' my friend said. 'I wonder how many more there are.'

'Too many.'

'Any is too many.'

We disposed of the body and went on. After a while, we came to a valley cutting through the hills. I could see part of an unpaved track. The track followed the fall of the ground until it disappeared from sight.

'Here we go,' my friend said. 'That will lead to a road. Now we're in business.'

Indeed, we were in business. It just seemed a pity that our business was killing.

8. The Empty Land

A pick-up truck and a station wagon – the monastery's entire transport fleet – stood outside the gate. Both were old but well-kept.

'We'll take the pick-up,' Philip said. 'It'll hold more loot.'

There was a trailer holding plastic oil drums attached to the back of the truck. When they climbed into the cab, Stephen was startled to see a double-barrelled shotgun secured by clips to the top of the backrest.

'You keep guns here?' he asked Philip.

'We use them to scare off vermin in the fields. We're not allowed to kill them, believe it or not.'

Stephen didn't like the gun. He liked it even less when Philip broke it open, took the cartridges out and replaced them with fresh ones.

'Why are you doing that?' Stephen asked.

'There's only birdshot in the old ones,' Philip said. 'These new ones will pack a wee bit more punch.'

'Are you expecting danger?'

The monk eyed him thoughtfully.

'It never hurts to be prepared,' he replied.

As they drove off, Stephen looked back at the monastery.

From the outside, it looked more like a fort than a house of religion. Seeing him looking, Kirsten told him it was very old. It had been abandoned for centuries before the monks revived it.

Stephen could see the new stonework where thc walls had been restored. The abbey lay in the heart of the mountains, standing on the crest of a low hill that was dwarfed by surrounding peaks. The top of the hill – it was hardly more than a mound – was almost flat, and on the gentle slopes outside the abbey walls an orchard of young apple trees shared space with wilder growth. A gravelled roadway led down from the gates, bridging a stream at the foot of the mound. As they crossed it, Philip pointed out the screen of evergreens hiding the little mountain lake from which the stream flowed. The lake was fed by the same underground springs as the monastery well. Philip explained that the little lake had been famous as a holy place long before Christianity existed. Its waters were believed to cure sickness, and even during the centuries of the monastery's ruin it had been visited for religious and superstitious reasons by local peasants.

'There's a thorn bush by the lake,' Philip said, 'and we still find offerings of rags tied to it sometimes. You never see anyone there, but you find the rags.'

The hills here weren't altogether bare, but they weren't cultivated either. It was a wild landscape. Stephen remembered that the monks had a farm, but he could see no sign of it. He asked Philip where the monastery fields were. Philip laughed.

'Bless you, boy,' he said, 'they're not up here! We bought

land, but there was no chance of getting it all in one piece, never mind getting it nearby. Land in these mountains is largely useless – unless you're a goat. Good land is scarce in these parts, so people hold on to it for generations. No, the monastery fields are scattered for miles – I think there's only two that border on each other. I only thank God that this didn't happen during the harvest – we'd never have coped.'

They'd turned from the gravelled track out on to a small dirt road. Stephen sat in silence for a while, looking out. The countryside did look empty, but then it looked like the kind of land that would be empty at the best of times. Millennia of storms from the Atlantic had washed most of the thin soil from the rocks. He saw why Philip had laughed at his question, this wasn't crop land, nor even grazing land – it was barren wilderness.

'It must be really weird out here now,' he said.

'No so much around here,' Philip said. 'Or at least no more than usual. Around here it's always this empty. But it felt very strange in the village we visited. Very strange altogether.'

'Strange?'

'Empty. It was empty. All the houses open, all the peoples' belongings still there – even their clothes.'

'Their clothes?'

'It looks like they all left in the middle of the night, dressed in whatever they slept in. It's like they all just ... vanished.'

Once they'd left the steepest, rawest hills behind they did start to pass a few cultivated fields. They even started to see living things apart from birds: a few rough mountain sheep at first and then, as the land improved, cattle. Through the open windows of the little truck Stephen heard a new sound, the first noise he'd heard apart from the sound of the truck itself. It was a strange pained lowing, an uncanny thing. Stephen thought of the old man's howling the night before.

'That's the cattle,' Philip said, seeing his puzzled look. 'They haven't been milked for days, and they don't like it. But there's nothing we can do for them – there's just too many and they're too scattered.'

They began to pass the occasional house now, small cottages and bungalows, or farmhouses with yards and outbuildings. After a while they turned off the little road on to a larger one. At the junction of the two roads stood several buildings, one of them a pub. The doors of the bar stood wide open to the weather.

'Look at that,' Philip said. 'There's proof that something very strange is going on – what Irish publican would leave his doors open like that?'

The new road brought them out of the mountains and through a series of dwindling hills. Still the vast emptiness went on. They saw all sorts of animals, but no people.

'It's weird,' Stephen said. 'It's just … weird. But at the same time it seems almost exciting. You feel you could do *anything*!'

'Yes,' Kirsten said. 'You're right. But it's all so scary – the emptiness.'

Philip smiled.

'Some people in the abbey,' he said, 'would think this was an improvement.'

'Like who?'

'Brother Simon, for instance.'

'Simon? But he's very polite. A bit sour maybe.' She looked at Stephen. 'Have you met him yet?'

Stephen supposed that, since there were only three monks, Simon must be the older monk who'd first found him awake.

'Seen,' he said. 'Not met.'

Philip laughed.

'Just as he'd like it,' he said. 'He's not overly fond of people. Or at least, he doesn't think much of them. Mind you, he has little cause to.'

'What happened to him?' Kirsten asked.

Philip thought for a while before answering.

'Do you know anything about our order?' he asked.

'Only what you've told me,' Kirsten said. 'That it's a multi-faith lay order founded after the last world war.'

'Yes. But it's more than just multi-faith – it's made up of all faiths and none. We have humanists, agnostics and atheists, the lot. And the order wasn't just set up *after* the war, it was set up in large part *because* of it – as a reaction to its horrors. By now, they have a whole string of monasteries scattered across the emptier parts of Europe, several in America, even a couple in North Africa. They buy old, ruined monasteries when they can and restore them. It's by no means a poor order, though we all live simply.'

'Where does the money come from?' Stephen asked.

'Bequests and gifts, mainly. Some of the richest European families send their sons to the monks for a few years of the contemplative life before they go "out in the world", as the order calls it. But what I was going to say is that the order wasn't always rich. When it was first set up, it was a terrible time in Europe. The whole continent was in ruins, and not just physically. People had found out about the things the Nazis did – the camps, the genocide. Evil, as Paul explained it to me, wasn't just a word anymore. Evil had a name and a face, and often it was your neighbour's face, or your brother's. Our order was founded by people who wanted to think about that, to make sense of it. Men joined for a few years or for a lifetime. When you meet some of the original monks – Simon is one – they're people who lived through terrible things. Simon was in the Dutch resistance and he had some very nasty experiences as a result of his involvement. He was betrayed by his own family, and he was tortured.'

'But what do the monks actually *do*?' Stephen asked. 'Set up abbeys in wild places and … think about evil?'

'Well, yes, basically that's exactly what we do.'

'And you? Where do you fit into this? Are you the son of a rich family?'

Philip hesitated.

'No,' he said finally, 'no, I'm not. You might say I'm an experiment of Paul's. I–'

Suddenly Philip braked hard, throwing the truck into a skid. The trailer slewed violently. When the truck came to a stop, Kirsten and Stephen stared at Philip, whose hands had gone white on the wheel. He, in turn, stared fixedly out of the driver's side-window.

'What is it?' Kirsten demanded.

Philip ignored her. His hand disappeared among the folds of his habit and drew out a big black pistol. Stephen felt the hairs on his neck twitch as he stared at the gun. He could understand that the monks might keep shotguns to frighten off vermin, but this was a weapon that no monk should ever have a use for. It was a tool for killing.

Philip opened the door of the truck and began to get out. He glanced back at them, his face icy. The change in him was complete.

'Stay here,' he said tightly. There were no laughs now. He got out, leaving the door open behind him, and set off back down the road. Stephen and Kirsten exchanged a look. Then, without saying a word, they both followed, Stephen hurrying, Kirsten reluctant.

9. The Victim in the Field

When Stephen reached Philip he was standing in front of a five-barred wooden gate, staring into the field beyond. The pistol hung forgotten in his hand. When Stephen's eyes followed the big monk's stare he saw what Philip's sharp eyes had spotted in passing – a bright patch of colour on the grass. Stephen had an awful suspicion that he knew what he was looking at. He heard Kirsten's light footfalls on the roadway behind him.

'Fräulein Herzenweg doesn't need to see this,' Philip said quietly. His voice was flat and strained. The patch of colour might have been a bundle of old rags, but it lay in a suspiciously human-looking mound. A white top, jeans and white skin where a face and two hands should be. The bundle was surrounded by a swarming cloud of flies.

Stephen turned away just as Kirsten reached him. He put himself between her and the gate and grabbed her arms.

'Philip wants us back in the truck,' he said.

Kirsten stared over his shoulder into the field. Her face was white and he could feel her trembling.

'That's a body,' she said. 'A person.'

'Come on,' Stephen said. 'We can do no good here.'

She let him lead her slowly back along the road. Kirsten

walked like a robot, guided by his arms around her shoulders. He felt goosebumps on her bare arms where his hands touched her skin. She was ice-cold in the summer heat. When they got to the pick-up she got in and sat there, staring straight ahead, hugging her knees, making no sound. Stephen felt he should at least try to say something comforting, but he couldn't think of anything. He was sorry about that, he could have used a bit of comfort himself.

Suddenly, sitting there in the bright sunlight, Stephen wasn't sure whether any of this was really happening. He no longer knew what was real and what was not. It all seemed impossible. He half-expected the whole scene to disappear, like the image of Kirsten by the well. He reached out and touched the round edges of the dashboard, feeling the smooth plastic surface with his fingertips. It felt dull enough to be real.

'Have you wondered,' he asked Kirsten, 'whether you might be dreaming all this?'

She looked at him. He was embarrassed. It sounded stupid when you said it out loud – though no more stupid, really, than the notion that everyone else in the entire world had somehow just *disappeared*.

'Right now I wish that I was,' she said. 'But we can't *both* be dreaming it. If I'm dreaming it then none of you are real. And if *you're* dreaming it ...'

She stopped short.

'That could have been me in that field!' she burst out. 'Or you!'

She shook her head.

'It's too crazy!' she said. 'It's all too crazy!'

She buried her head in her knees and started to sob. Her shoulders shook. It was hard to believe that this terrified child was the same happy girl who'd set out so excitedly this morning. Then she'd been hungry to see what might be out here in this brave new world. Now she'd seen it. She had seen that the new world had teeth and claws, and used them.

'Maybe it was an accident or something,' Stephen said weakly.

Kirsten shook her head without raising it.

'You know that's not so,' her muffled voice said. 'Something is out here. Something dangerous. And we're out here, too.'

Stephen felt he should put his arm around her or something – try to comfort her somehow. But he felt shy about doing it, and he couldn't think of anything comforting to say that wouldn't be a barefaced lie. So they both sat there, miserably. After a while, Kirsten stopped crying.

'I'm being childish,' she said firmly. 'Whatever is happening, crying won't help. We have to be sensible.'

She dried her eyes with a big, white handkerchief she pulled from her sleeve.

Philip returned and called Stephen. He looked dazed and appalled. There was no sign of the big pistol now. Philip brought Stephen to the back of the truck and spoke in low tones that Kirsten couldn't hear.

'I may as well tell you now,' he said. 'It was a man. He's been killed.'

'By animals?'

'You could say that, but they walked on two legs. They were human — after their fashion.'

Stephen looked at him.

'We can't just leave him lying there,' Philip said. 'We need to bury him. We have shovels here in the truck. But I'll be all day digging a proper grave on my own.'

'I'll help you,' Stephen said.

'Good man. I hoped you'd offer. But I have to warn you, he's not a pretty sight. Whoever killed him enjoyed the work. They liked hurting people.'

Stephen felt his stomach churning.

'I don't care,' he said. 'I'll still do it. It's like you say — we can't just leave him there.'

Philip looked at him steadily, then nodded again.

'Good,' he said.

There was a recessed handle in the floor of the pick-up truck. Philip pulled it up to reveal a storage compartment for tools. He took out two broad-bladed shovels and handed one to Stephen.

'Let's get this over with,' he said, 'before we lose our nerve.'

But it didn't come to that — at least, not in the way Philip meant. What happened instead was, if possible, even more unnerving.

When they got to the gate Stephen avoided looking into the field. He was afraid of what he'd see. He knew he'd have to look at it, but he didn't want to see it any sooner than he had to.

Philip started to climb over the gate, but then stopped.

'God almighty,' he breathed.

In spite of himself, Stephen looked. There was nothing to see. The place where the body had been was empty. Philip jumped down inside the field and ran to the spot, with Stephen following. Philip stared around, wild-eyed, unable to speak. The long grass should at least have been crushed where the body had lain, but it wasn't. There was no sign that anything heavier than the air had pressed it down. Even the flies were gone. Philip let out a long, hissing breath between his teeth. He whimpered like a child. His eyes rolled, frightened and frightening, in his head. He was a terrified man. Stephen knew exactly how he felt.

'Oh my sweet saviour!' Philip hissed. 'What devil's work is this?'

10. Agents on the Road

My friend and I followed the mountain track down through the hills. After a while we came to a crossroads where the track joined a wider, paved road. There was a house there, a prosperous-looking bungalow with a gravelled yard surrounded by a low stone wall. The front door of the house was open, and there was a car parked in the yard.

'There you go,' my friend said. 'Transport. Dirty old things, cars, but they have their uses.'

He vaulted the low wall and landed on the gravel in the yard. I followed him. The car was unlocked and we went into the house to look for the ignition keys. In the livingroom a half-grown cat howled at us hungrily. My friend invited it into the kitchen to look for some food. I searched for the keys and found them in the bedroom, on a locker beside the rumpled bed. I went back to the kitchen, where the cat was twining itself around my friend's legs. He'd found a can of food with a picture of a cat on its label, and was trying to figure out how to operate the ring-pull.

'It's terrible to see all these dependent animals,' he sighed.

'Look on the bright side,' I said. 'At least the humans haven't wiped these ones out too.'

My friend finally got the can open and poured the food into a bowl.

'I'm not sure how bright a side that is,' he said. 'I'd hate to be depending on humans for *my* survival.'

We watched the little animal wolf down the food. It growled fiercely as it ate.

'I've never understood,' my friend said, 'how cats let themselves be fooled by humans. I mean, dogs are born idiots, but you'd think cats would have more sense — or at least more self-respect.'

Suddenly the cat did one of those reverse feline jumps. It arched its back and its fur stood on end, and it bared its teeth and hissed. It was staring at the window. I looked at my friend. He met my eyes and smiled.

'Bad guys,' he said. 'Outside. I felt them too.' He sighed. 'Ho hum,' he said. 'No rest for the wicked.'

He led the way to the front door. We went out with the crystals already in our hands. They came at us as soon as we emerged, two young boys as crazed as the one we'd already unshaded. These two, like him, were ragged and dirty. They were just as stupid too. They ran straight at us, screaming and growling and snapping. My friend unshaded both of them without even breaking step.

'So they even attack us,' he said with mild interest. 'Things really have got out of hand here, haven't they?'

He sighed again.

'Interfering amateurs,' he said, 'are a pain in the neck.'

We left them lying in the yard and drove away.

'Which way?' my friend asked.

I stroked my crystal. It was cool now, neutral.

'I don't know,' I said. 'We've a lot of ground to cover. The nearest town first, I suppose. Maybe we can pick up a trail. We have to start somewhere.'

The fact that we couldn't trace the people we were looking for wasn't reassuring. We'd tried everything before coming ourselves. I didn't want to dwell on the possibilities, so when my friend drove the car out onto the road I concentrated on the scenery. It was pleasant in the car, driving through the heat with open windows, watching the bare hills and fields streaming by. There was a tape-player in the dash, and after checking aimlessly through some cassettes that were beside it I stuck one at random into the machine and switched it on. The music of the country came softly through the speakers, a wild, sad, lonesome music made by pipes and whistles and stringed things. I listened to it as I enjoyed the view, feeling the breeze wash over the skin of my face. The sun was moving slowly lower in the sky.

'Their music moves me sometimes,' I said to my friend. 'It's hard to believe that it's made by them at all.'

He nodded at the tape machine.

'That stuff there,' he said, 'comes out of the place itself. They're just a channel for it.'

At the next crossroads there was a signpost giving directions and distances. My friend turned in the direction of the closest indicated town. When we reached it, we saw it was hardly worthy of the name. It was a small collection of houses at yet another crossroads. We stopped by a tourist shop, and my friend got out and tried the handle of the door. It wasn't locked and he went in. I stayed in the car and listened to the lonely music. I didn't bother keeping watch. The place was deserted – I could feel it in my borrowed bones.

My friend came back with a large-scale tourist map of the area and spread it out across the warm bonnet of the car. I got out and joined him. He took out a pencil he'd also borrowed, a gaudy thing that said *Welcome to Ireland!*

'Indeed,' I thought, reading it.

With the pencil my friend traced a rough outline of the exclusion zone on the map. Inside the barrier there would be nobody except our kind, broadly speaking. Within the rough circle he'd marked, the map showed half a dozen settlements. None were very big. It was a sparsely populated area – too bare and mountainous to sustain any large communities.

'Do you remember this area at all?' he asked.

'Not really. Why? Is there something special about it?'

'Oh yes, at least there used to be, a long time ago. Something *very* special.'

I looked at the map, trying to see through the changes that millennia of man and weather had wrought. Suddenly I saw it.

'The crystal works!' I said.

My friend nodded, pointing to a place on the map.

'There,' he said. 'In those mountains.'

The land he indicated lay further to the north. The road that we were on would eventually bring us there. I pointed to a tiny patch of blue.

'That must be the birthing lake,' I said.

I felt a sort of sadness run through me. My hand went absentmindedly into my coat pocket to stroke the crystal. It had been formed here, in the bowels of that little patch of blue. The stone bones of the hills and the cold humours of the waters had joined in its making, once upon a time before time.

'Do you think it's a coincidence?' I asked my friend. 'It must be. These hills are dead now.'

'Or sleeping,' he said. He shrugged. 'Time will tell. Our best bet now is to go that way, though. There's a town up there that looks fairly big. Maybe we'll find something there.'

He folded the map. I was lost in thought. Imagine forgetting the place you'd been made – even after so long. For the first time in my life I felt old, though I was young in the eyes of my people. My friend read my mind.

'What's a thousand years between friends?' he said. It was a saying we had.

11. The Stiff Upper Lip

On the way back to the truck Stephen suggested that they say nothing to Kirsten about the disappearing body.

'She's upset enough as it is,' he said.

Philip seemed to be still in shock. His eyes were less wild, but he looked at Stephen as though he'd never seen him before. It seemed to take him a while to understand what the boy had said.

'Yes,' he said. 'You're right. And whatever happened back there, we have to keep control of ourselves. At least I do.'

He smiled. It looked sad and forced and completely artificial, but Stephen was glad to see it nonetheless. For a while he'd thought Philip was losing it completely.

Philip took several deep breaths.

'I'm not even going to wonder what happened back there,' he said.

By the time they reached the pick-up truck the big monk had regained at least some semblance of composure. So – to Stephen's surprise – had Kirsten. She had the air of someone who'd given herself a good talking to. Her face was pale, but there was no sign of the tears she'd cried earlier except some redness around her eyes.

Stephen and Philip got back into the truck. Philip turned the key in the ignition, but then he paused and turned to them.

'Look,' he said, his voice trembling slightly, 'there's no use in pretending. There's a killer about. Killers. They may be near, they may not be. They may be dangerous to us, they may not be. We have to assume that they are. I'm not happy having you two out here. I think maybe I should take you both back to the abbey.'

'No!'

Kirsten's reaction was immediate. Stephen was taken aback by the change in her. She looked positively angry.

'I'm not a baby, Philip,' she said. 'So now we know it's dangerous out here. All right. But anywhere is dangerous – a city street is dangerous if it's the wrong street and the wrong time. We can go back to the abbey, but the abbey will still need the supplies we came to get. So you'll only have to make another trip. We must be near the town by now, right?'

'We're almost there.'

'So let's do what we came to do. There are three of us. We have guns.'

She looked at Stephen, who was staring at her in amazement

'I *refuse* to be terrified!' she said. 'Even if this is a dream, I refuse to let it be a nightmare!'

Philip stared at her too.

'She's right,' he said softly. There was a tinge of admiration in his voice. 'We have work to do.'

But he didn't sound too happy about it. Philip couldn't

altogether hide how uneasy he felt. But he put his foot on the pedal and they set off.

'Stiff upper lip, eh, Fräulein Herzenweg?' Philip said.

Kirsten pushed her top lip out and flattened it. She looked so silly even Stephen smiled.

'Stiff upper lip, Brother Philip,' Kirsten said.

Stephen said nothing. He'd been watching Philip's eyes in the driver's mirror. The wild look he'd seen in them back in the field had frightened him at least as much as the body and its mysterious disappearance. The eyes were masked now, carefully controlled, but he imagined he could still see a hint of that mad gleam in their depths. And there was still the little matter of the pistol: what exactly was a monk doing with a gun like that? Philip had held the gun with an easy familiarity – he'd obviously handled pistols before.

There were too many mysteries here by far for Stephen's liking.

12. The Market Town

The town was large by local standards only. A long string of buildings on either side of the road made up the main street. Four or five sidestreets stretched off it for short distances on either side. They drove in slowly and watchfully. The place looked deserted. There weren't even any dogs in the streets. Most of the doors in the houses stood open and there were cars and vans parked neatly on both sides of the road. A light breeze toyed idly with dust and discarded bits of paper.

Kirsten peered carefully at each building as they passed by. Reaching the town seemed to have cheered her up – at least, if she was acting it was a very convincing act. She seemed almost her old excited self, and when they passed the first super-market she gave a little squeal of delight.

'A supermarket!' she said. 'I never thought I'd be so glad to see one!'

About halfway down its length, the street widened into a central square that was also a crossroads. In the centre of the square stood a statue commemorating some war of liberation or other. Philip parked close to the statue and everyone got out. The silence was eerier here in the town. It was no longer natural.

Philip had drawn the pistol again and was holding it like he meant business. Kirsten was busying herself with the big notebook, checking her shoplifting list. She headed straight for a chemist's shop she'd spotted in the square, with the expression of a desert wanderer sighting an oasis. When she tried the door, it opened. The other two watched her go in.

'We'll have to split up for at least part of this,' Philip said to Stephen. 'I don't like it, but it's the quickest way, and the sooner we're back in the abbey the happier I'll be.'

'I'll stick with Kirsten, then,' Stephen said. 'Maybe I should take the shotgun.'

'Yes,' Philip said. 'I wanted to talk to you about that. You don't mind carrying a weapon?'

'I do mind. But I'd feel better, under the circumstances.'

Philip nodded. He put his hand into the pocket of his robe, then took it out and held it, palm upwards, out to Stephen. Lying in his hand was a little silver-coloured automatic pistol.

'Take this,' he said. 'It's easier to carry than a shotgun. There's not much of a punch to it, but if you shoot anything with it they'll know that they're hit.'

Stephen stared at the wicked-looking little gun. It was only a baby thing compared with the big pistol Philip carried, but it was a real gun nonetheless. So, Philip had two pistols – *at least* two pistols. It was very strange that he should have one; that he should have more was positively bizarre.

He looked up again into Philip's face. The monk was

watching his reaction carefully. Stephen badly wanted to know what was going through his mind, but there was no way to tell. He took the proffered weapon.

'We'll find most of what we need either in the supermarket or in the cash and carry,' Philip said. 'We should do those together. We can pick up the fuel we need from the petrol station on the way back. But there's a hardware shop around the corner where I need to get some things. So I'd like you and Fräulein Herzenweg to do a job for Paul while I do that.'

'Of course. What is it?'

'I want you and the Fräulein to go to the library.'

Stephen blinked at him in disbelief. The *library*? A Viking raid for *library books*?

Philip pointed at a venerable-looking building that took up one side of the square.

'In there,' he said. 'Up the stairs. You can't miss it.'

'But–'

Philip held his hands up in front of him.

'Don't blame me,' he said. 'It's Paul's idea. He's a great man for books, is Paul. He asked me specifically to get you two to do the job. Maybe he thinks it's the safest place for you – I don't think Paul believes *anything* dangerous can happen in a library.'

Stephen was still looking at him in disbelief.

'There are two black plastic bags under your seat in the truck,' Philip said. 'You take them in, and you fill them with books – a selection. It's very straightforward.'

Stephen shrugged. The idea seemed daft, but to tell the

truth he quite fancied the idea of being in a place where nothing dangerous could happen. Or at least of keeping Kirsten in a place like that.

'Whatever you say,' he said.

Philip looked at him, considering. Suddenly he lowered his voice and spoke urgently, finally showing his masked unease nakedly.

'Listen,' he said. 'That body back there.'

Stephen had been trying not to think about that body. Here in this very ordinary town – even if it was deserted – dead bodies seemed a long way away.

'Yes?'

'It wasn't … *right.*'

Stephen wasn't sure what he meant. The body had been murdered, of course that wasn't right.

'In what way, *not right?*'

'It was all cut up, stabbed and slashed. But there was no blood.'

'No blood?'

'Not a drop.'

'You mean something had drained it all out?'

'I don't know. Maybe it was hacked about after it was dead – you don't bleed when you're dead. But even then there'd be *something,* some stain or something. *But there was nothing.* You'd have got more blood out of a tailor's dummy.'

'But isn't that weird?'

'*Weird?* It's impossible! But that's how it was.'

'What could it mean?' Stephen asked.

'All I can think of,' Philip said, 'is that the body wasn't human. It was … something else.'

Stephen stared at him blankly.

'Something else?'

'Don't ask me what, because I don't know. But between the lack of blood and the way it just disappeared … I can't believe it was human at all.'

'But what was it then?'

Philip snorted. 'If I knew that,' he said, 'I'd be a happier man.'

Stephen looked down at the little silver gun. It wasn't a toy, he reminded himself, even though it looked like one. He was frightened of the unknown threat now abroad in the world, but he was almost more frightened of the gun. Then he thought of Kirsten. He couldn't leave her undefended because of his squeamishness.

'Don't use that unless you really need to,' Philip said. 'But if you do need to use it, then don't hesitate. Your life might depend on it. More than your life, in fact.'

'More?'

'Yes,' Philip said. 'Mine.'

Stephen shivered. But before he could say anything else Kirsten reappeared from the chemist's. She carried two big plastic bags full of booty, which she swung with real pleasure. Looking at her grinning face, Stephen thought of the dead body in the field. He was suddenly glad that he'd taken the gun.

13. The Assault in the Library

Kirsten threw her loot into the pick-up truck and joined them. She wasn't too happy at first with the job Philip wanted them to do. She was like a little child who'd been let loose in a toyshop only to be told, just as she was getting into the swing of things, that it was time to go home and do her homework. But she cheered up when Philip promised they'd have time to raid more interesting shops later.

'I think I could get to like thieving,' she said with a grin.

They fetched the plastic sacks from the car, while Philip set off to the hardware shop.

'Any special book requests?' Kirsten called after the big monk. When he looked back you could see his white teeth grinning through the black curls of his beard. The grin looked genuine, and again Stephen felt uneasy – either the man was a great actor or his moods were all over the place.

'Just don't get anything too steamy,' joked Philip. 'We don't want too many distractions.'

Then he was gone, and they crossed the square to the library.

'I'd really much rather be doing a bit of pillaging,' Kirsten complained.

'With any luck,' Stephen pointed out, 'we won't even get in.'

But there was nothing to stop them. The door of the building was old and solid-looking, but it stood slightly ajar. Stephen wasn't sure he liked that. The disappearances seemed to have happened late on Sunday night, a time when library doors should be locked. It suggested that someone had been here since then.

The door swung open at a push, and they were in a large front hall. Before them was a broad staircase. Off the hall were anonymous offices, most of them identical and all of them empty. The quietness seemed even quieter here.

'Now this is *really* creepy,' Kirsten whispered. It was a whispering sort of place.

They went up the stairs, their footsteps echoing in the stairwell. In front of them, on the next landing, stood a glass door with the words *Public Library* written on it in gilt letters. They stopped, hesitant. They looked at each other with embarrassed smiles.

'Robbing a library,' Kirsten whispered. 'It feels almost sinful!'

But she didn't sound as though that bothered her. Her whisper echoed, as though a mocking little voice was aping hers.

For a moment they both just stood outside the door. Even now Stephen half expected a librarian to appear, demanding to know what they were at. Then the sound of breaking glass came from somewhere outside, startling them.

'There goes the hardware shop,' Stephen said.

The noise had broken the spell. Stephen shrugged off his unease and pushed at the library door. It swung open.

The library was a single, large, rectangular room. Big windows that looked out on to the square took up most of the wall straight ahead. The other walls were covered with bookshelves. Free-standing bookstacks stood scattered around the carpeted floor. Stephen felt himself relax. Inside the library the silence seemed less oppressive. It suited the place: you expected libraries to be quiet.

Immediately in front of them stood an old-fashioned glass-fronted library counter with low wooden gates on either side of it marked *In* and *Out*. Kirsten, bubbling at the opportunity, breezed in through the gate marked *Out*. Stephen used the proper gate. They stood looking around.

'You start at that end,' Kirsten said, pointing. 'And I'll start over here. We'll meet in the middle.'

They started filling the plastic sacks, working in silence. Stephen noticed that Kirsten examined each book before selecting or replacing it. He himself flitted from shelf to shelf, picking titles that caught his eye. As he rounded the free-standing stack furthest from the door, he noticed that the room wasn't, as he'd thought, perfectly rectangular. There was a walk-in alcove at this end. A sign above it read *Reference Section*. At the back of the alcove was another door. Set in its top half was a window of cloudy frosted glass. As he looked at the glass, Stephen thought he saw a shadow behind it – a moving shadow.

He stood stock-still, waiting. A shiver ran up his spine.

There was no sound. He wasn't even sure he'd really seen anything. He looked back at Kirsten, but she was still busy selecting books. Should he say something, and risk looking like an idiot when the room turned out to be empty?

He looked back at the door, licking lips that were suddenly very dry. There was no sign of movement. Stephen cursed himself for a panicky fool. The eyes play tricks when things are tense. The hairs were tingling on his neck, but he'd heard nothing and seen ... what? A movement that might have been anything or nothing. The shadow of a window-blind blowing in the breeze.

But there was no breeze.

'Get a hold of yourself,' he told himself.

He walked boldly over to the door in the alcove and put his hand on the knob. It turned easily and the door opened inwards. But before he could open it fully the knob was yanked from his hand, and something hit him very hard in the face.

Stephen toppled backwards, and as he fell he was hit again, hard, in the shoulder, by what felt like a boot. Someone flung himself on top of him. Blows were aimed at his head, and he had just enough sense to throw his arms up in front of his face. Several pairs of running feet went by him. His arms took the worst of the heavy blows, but some of them landed. He was dazed. Little stars sparked and died in front of his eyes. His attacker was growling, a savage sound that didn't sound human at all. Stephen felt sick to his stomach with fear. He thought of the body in the field. He felt he was going to pass out.

Then Kirsten screamed.

The sound seemed to trip a strange switch inside Stephen. There was a very peculiar feeling in his head, a sudden twisting, *pulling* sensation, as though his mind itself was trying to escape from his body. For a moment he had a feeling that was very hard to describe: it was almost as though he – not his body, but *he* – was somewhere else entirely. Then his mind seemed to snap back into his body like a piece of over-stretched elastic suddenly released.

He was instantly very alert and very aware. Everything seemed very, very clear. His body moved as though with a will of its own. His hands caught his attacker's wrists, his speed surprising both of them. Stephen saw the other's face for the first time. It was the face of a boy not much older than himself, a dirty face twisted into a look of utter hatred. The youth's teeth were bared in a doglike snarl, and Stephen shuddered as he saw that they were sharp, as though they'd been filed. Thick spit was drooling from his mouth. The boy's eyes were dark and burning. He was very strong, but Stephen didn't feel weak now at all. He held the youth's hands easily, then bucked his hips so that the bigger boy was thrown off him. Stephen let go of his wrists and his attacker flew helplessly through the air and slammed into the wall with an explosive grunt. He fell on the ground with a cascade of displaced library books raining down on him.

Stephen was already on his feet, reaching for the little pistol he'd put in his back pocket. Hearing footsteps behind him, he pulled the pistol, swung round and used the gun to clout another youth who'd almost reached him. The gun hit his skull with a hollow pop. The youth gave an animal yelp and fell to the floor. Stephen swung again to face his first attacker, but he was still lying on the floor, groaning in pain, his hands making weak flapping movements. The second attacker lay on the floor, unmoving.

Stephen turned to where he'd last seen Kirsten. She was struggling with two more youths, their faces as crazily twisted as those of the ones who'd attacked him. These too were growling in no human way. One of them stood behind Kirsten, his arm around her throat. The second was in front of her, and as Stephen watched Kirsten gave him a round-house kick in the stomach. Even the sight of it made Stephen wince. The youth made a sound like a punctured air-cushion and jack-knifed forward. He swivelled away and stood doubled up in front of one of the big windows, his back turned to Kirsten. Kirsten bent her leg and planted her foot square in the small of his back. She pushed.

The boy never knew what hit him. He shot forward and smashed through the glass. The low ledge caught his legs below the knees, and then, with a squeal, he was gone.

Kirsten and Stephen stared wide-eyed at the smashed, empty window. But the other attackers seemed hardly to notice that they'd lost a companion. Someone – one of the two youths he'd already downed – jumped on Stephen from behind, dragging him to the floor. He lay face down with the weight of his assailant on his back. A clawed hand gripped the wrist of his gun-holding hand. Another grabbed the back of his neck, grinding his face into the spiky carpet. Stephen struggled uselessly. Then a second body smashed down on top of him, knocking all his breath out. A rain of punches started falling on his head and back. Consciousness began to slip away.

'Kirsten!' he screamed, his voice muffled by the carpet. '*Run*!'

But he had no idea whether or not she was in any position to obey.

I'm going to die here, he thought with a strange calmness, without even knowing who I really am.

There was a loud hollow bang. The weight on Stephen's back suddenly shifted. There was a second bang, a sharper, cracking sound, and part of the weight went away. The hands on his wrist and neck disappeared. He started to scramble to his feet, waiting to be hit again. Only as he stood upright did he look around.

Philip stood inside the library gate with his big black pistol raised. Wisps of shifting blue smoke curled in the still air.

The last of Kirsten's attackers lay sprawled on the floor by the window. Kirsten herself stood staring down at him with huge terrified eyes. When Stephen looked around he saw one of his own attackers lying deathly still. The last attacker, the one he'd originally thrown against the wall, stood snarling at Philip. The snarl showed his wicked teeth. The boy reached into his pocket and took something out. A knife's long thin blade flicked out with a click, and he brandished it at Stephen.

'Ten,' he said, or something that sounded like it: Tern?

Teln? The boy's voice sounded as though there was something wrong with his throat.

Stephen held up his own little gun helplessly. He knew he couldn't use it.

'Shoot!' Philip said loudly. 'Shoot!'

The boy didn't shift his gaze. He stared at Stephen with a hatred in his eyes that seemed almost personal.

Do I know you? Stephen wondered. Do you know me? He felt a terrible longing to ask it aloud.

With a scream the youth jumped towards him. There was another bang, the sound of Philip firing. The boy performed an impossible mid-air somersault, as though plucked at by some giant invisible hand. He was flung to the ground, limp, like a discarded piece of old rag, and lay without moving.

Stephen still held the pistol out in front of him. He could see his hand shaking wildly. Then his whole body started shaking. He saw Philip walk over to the body. He extended his foot carefully and rolled it over. The corpse flopped onto its back. Philip stared at it. Then he turned to Stephen and raised his arm. Stephen found himself looking down the barrel of the big black pistol. He looked up at Philip's face. It was as white as a sheet. His eyes were even more wild than they'd been back in the field. There was sweat on his forehead. He was shaking almost as much as Stephen. Stephen knew he was about to shoot him. For the second time in minutes he was sure he was going to die. He looked down again at the pistol's muzzle. It made a third eye, looking at him, a black and wicked little eye, but still one saner than the eyes in Philip's head.

'No blood,' Philip said in a strangled voice. 'Three of them shot. One of them fallen twenty feet onto concrete and not a single drop of blood between them.'

Stephen's shaking grew wilder and wilder. He felt curiously distant from himself. His knees trembled. Then he keeled over and everything went away.

14. Agents in Pursuit

The second village we came to was bigger than the first. According to the map it was the biggest settlement within the exclusion zone. It had a market square in the centre, and in the square there was a body lying on the ground. My friend parked the car by a statue of a young man with a gun in his hands and we got out very carefully, our crystals drawn.

The body was dead. Looking up, we could see a smashed window in the top floor of the building before which it lay. Taken with the drift of glass shards scattered around the sprawled figure, it explained the cause of the boy's death. Except, of course, that it wasn't a boy. It wasn't one of our creatures either – it was a hunter.

We went inside warily. The building was deserted. The room with the broken window turned out to be a library. There were three more dead hunters there. They'd all been shot. My friend and I looked at each other.

'Now this,' my friend said, 'is a fine how d'you do.'

'You think our people did it?'

'They must have – although I'd swear there'd been humans here recently.'

There were two big, black, plastic bags lying on the floor,

half-filled with library books. My friend looked at them, frowning. He shook his head.

'This *is* a puzzle,' he said.

'Could the hunters be fighting each other?'

'Anything's possible, I suppose. But what would hunters want with books? The Sug aren't what you'd call great readers. And I'd swear I could feel humans.'

'Well, it's a human town. The place was alive with them only a couple of days ago.'

He shrugged.

'Maybe,' he said doubtfully.

'We couldn't have … *overlooked* some humans in the clearance, could we?'

My friend winced.

'I don't even want to think about that,' he said.

I knew we'd found something significant, even if its significance eluded us.

I ran through the possibilities in my mind. One, the hunters were fighting amongst themselves. That was very good, it would leave us less to kill. Two, our own people, or some of the others, were still capable of fighting back. That was pretty good as well. Three, there were humans around. That was definitely *not* good. In fact, that was terrible. For a start it meant that the hunters were so crazy they might have attacked humans. That would be very bad news for all of us, because humans, as individuals, are not very robust.

'Let's get out of here,' I said to my friend. 'I'm getting a headache just thinking about it.'

He nodded.

'I'm starting to get a very bad feeling about all this,' he said.

'Really?' I asked. 'I've had a bad feeling about it all along.'

We got back into the car and drove out of town. We played no music now. After a while the road began to climb again, back into mountainous country. A few miles on I felt a special sort of strangeness. I looked over at my friend. He'd felt it too.

'Sug,' he said.

'Only one, I think.'

'The Hunt Lord most likely. I want to have a little chat with that idiot.'

Somehow I didn't think the Hunt Lord would enjoy the experience. My friend can get quite nasty when he's in a temper.

We saw him as we rounded a bend in the road. He was sitting on a fallen tree a little way up a slope, a big stout man in brown clothes. He showed no sign of alarm – if anything, he seemed to have been waiting for us. He rose to his feet when the car stopped. There could be no doubt that this was – in theory at least – the leader of the hunters. Although from what we'd seen it was obvious that he'd lost control of them. I felt anger rise in me, but it faded when I saw his pale drawn face approach the car. There was an odd mix of emotions competing to take control of that face. Tiredness, pain, and to my surprise something that might have been shame. Worry too. Most surprising of all was a flash, quickly suppressed, of something that looked awfully like relief.

When he reached the car the Sug leaned down and peered in through the open window.

'Am I glad to see you two!' he said.

That's when I knew that things were worse than I'd ever imagined.

15. The Phantom in the Supermarket

Stephen opened his eyes to find himself back in his bed in the abbey. He blinked in panic at the low ceiling. For a moment he wondered whether the whole trip to town had been a nightmare. But then he felt the aches in his body where he'd been punched and kicked.

The light in the room was dim and red. It was either dawn or evening. He raised his head. In the dimness he saw a tall thin figure sitting at the table: the abbot. The monk sat motionless, his elbow on the table, his sharp chin cupped in his hand, staring at the bed.

'Abbot Paul,' Stephen said weakly.

The abbot came over and sat on the bed.

'Relax,' he said softly. 'You're safe now.'

'What time is it? What day?'

'Saturday. Saturday morning. Dawn.'

Stephen blinked.

'I've been unconscious since yesterday afternoon?'

'I shouldn't worry. Your body obviously needed rest.'

He took matches from his habit and lit the candles in the candleholder. The soft light spread. Stephen saw that the abbot's face looked grave and tired.

'Have you been here long?' he asked.

Paul smothered a yawn.

'Since last night,' he said. 'I didn't want you to be alone when you woke up.'

'Is everybody all right?'

'Yes, I think so. But I need to talk to you.'

Stephen sat up, fully awake now. His body hurt. He felt it gingerly.

'There's nothing broken,' the abbot said. 'But you're rather bruised.'

'We were almost killed in that library,' Stephen said, the memory of it making him shiver. 'If Philip hadn't come when he did we'd have been finished.'

'Yes,' the abbot said, 'Philip's arrival. That's what I want to talk to you about.'

'He was in the nick of time. Another few seconds and …'

His voice trailed off in the face of the abbot's steady gaze. The tall monk was staring into Stephen's eyes as though trying to read his mind. The brown eyes locked with the boy's for what seemed like minutes. Then the abbot nodded slowly.

'You know nothing about it,' he said regretfully. 'That's a pity.'

'What should I know about? Those people attacked us. Kirsten pushed one out of the window – I don't think she meant to, but she did it. Then Philip came and shot the others. That's all I know. What more is there?'

The abbot looked at his hands and pursed his lips.

'Yesterday morning,' he said, 'when you came downstairs, you met a young novice. His name is Thomas.'

'Yes. He was scrubbing the floor. I startled him.'

'I know. Then you went to find Fräulein Herzenweg and Philip. In the courtyard, something happened to you.'

Stephen tried to remember.

'No. I mean yes, but nothing serious. I had a fit of weakness. I stopped by the well.'

'And?'

'And ... nothing. A little weakness, hardly surprising my first time out of bed. It passed, and I went looking for Kirsten.'

'After your party left the monastery,' the abbot said, 'Brother Thomas came to see me. He was very frightened, because he thought he was catching whatever it is that's wrong with the majority of our guests. He thought he was seeing things.'

'Seeing things? Like what? What did he see?'

'He saw ... he saw you stop by the well. Then you leaned over and looked down into the water. And just then, as Thomas watched, Fräulein Herzenweg appeared beside you – literally. She didn't walk over to you. She simply appeared, out of thin air, standing beside you and looking at you with some concern. You jumped up, obviously startled, and turned to look at her. But she was gone. She'd disappeared – like a light going out, Thomas said.'

Stephen felt the blood drain from his face.

'But that was a hallucination,' he said. 'I didn't mention it to anyone. I thought I mightn't be let go on the trip.'

'So. You did see it too. And do you think Brother Thomas shared your hallucination?'

'No. That's not possible. But Kirsten simply wasn't *in* the courtyard. She was with Philip.'

'I know,' Paul said. 'So when Thomas told me his story, I reassured him that he wasn't going mad and I told him to rest. The youngster is overwrought – we all are – and people see things when they're frightened. The mind under stress does peculiar things. But when I spoke to Philip yesterday before you left, he mentioned that Fräulein Herzenweg had a moment's faintness just before you came along. Perhaps she had, after all, gone outside to clear her head. Philip hadn't mentioned it, but then he didn't say that she didn't go out.'

Stephen could see that this latest mystery was cause for concern. Was there really some contagious form of madness loose in the world? What was it – an experimental weapon of some kind? But that would suggest that some terrible war really had broken out.

'You think the madness might be spreading?' he asked the abbot in a hushed voice.

Paul sighed.

'I haven't finished my story,' he said. 'I sent Thomas to rest, but of course I didn't dismiss his story – one can't dismiss any oddity in this situation. I just thought I'd check with you when you returned.'

'And?'

'Fräulein Herzenweg was with Philip when you and

Thomas saw her, there's no doubt about that. But she did report an odd passing weakness just before you came in. She described it as a strange *pulling* sensation in her head. She couldn't recall ever having such a feeling before – of course, that means nothing in the circumstances.'

Stephen frowned. 'But you're not taking seriously the notion that ...'

He stopped. What, if anything, was the abbot suggesting?

'When your party came back,' Paul continued gently, 'it was obvious that something very bad had happened. Philip said he had to talk to me immediately.'

He seemed unsure how to go on. He leaned forward and stared into Stephen's eyes again.

'I'm certain you're telling me the truth as you know it,' he said. 'And I'm equally sure about Fräulein Herzenweg. Tell me, the weakness you felt in the courtyard, did it feel in any way *odd*?'

'Odd? No. It was just a weakness.'

'And later? In the library? Did you have any peculiar feelings then?'

Stephen was getting angry. He wanted to retort that he'd had several peculiar feelings, mainly the certainty that he was going to be murdered. But then he thought of what Paul had just said about Kirsten's description of her weakness, a "strange pulling sensation in her head". He suddenly remembered the moment in the library when he'd heard Kirsten's scream, and the weird *twisting* sensation he'd felt in his own mind.

It had been a very odd feeling, but in the later excitement he'd forgotten it. Was the abbot suggesting that it was connected with that morning's hallucinations? Had something like that happened again – had someone else seen Kirsten? But the abbot seemed almost surprised when Stephen asked him that question.

'You're missing the point,' he said softly. 'Not Fräulein Herzenweg. Nobody saw *her*.'

And then Stephen realised what he was implying.

'Me?' he asked, almost choking on the word. 'Someone saw *me*?'

'After he left you, Philip went into a hardware shop. While he was there, he sensed someone behind him. When he turned, he saw you. You looked exactly as you had when he'd last seen you a couple of minutes before. He was annoyed that you'd managed to come up behind him without his noticing you. But he was worried because you were alone. You said nothing, but you gestured, beckoning him. He was looking right at you, and he saw what happened next.'

Stephen didn't want to say the words, but he was certain he knew what they were and he didn't want Paul to say them either.

'I disappeared?' he said in a small voice.

'You disappeared. Into thin air. Like a light going out. Philip overcame his shock and ran to the library. As he reached the square he saw one of your attackers come out through the library window. He ran upstairs. You saw the rest yourself.'

Stephen hung his head.

'You, of course,' Paul said, 'had never left the library.'

'No,' Stephen said. 'I hadn't.' He looked into the abbot's brown eyes. 'Paul, I knew nothing of this. I swear.'

The abbot nodded wearily.

'I believe you,' he said. 'In a way I was hoping that you did know something, however odd the explanation.'

Stephen stared at the quilt on the bed. His mind was numb. Paul tried to say something soothing.

'It's obviously some kind of *doppelgänger*,' he said. 'A double. I've heard of such things, though I must admit I always thought of them as legends. But there seems to be nothing threatening about it – quite the reverse, in fact. Your appearance yesterday saved your lives.'

'Yes,' said Stephen blankly. He was anything but convinced. It wasn't comfortable to think that another version of you was likely to appear somewhere without your knowing about it. And Stephen had no solid identity to hold on to: what if he himself turned out to be the double?

Mad thoughts maybe, but it wasn't the sanest of situations. In his mind Stephen saw again the wicked little eye of the gun-barrel staring at him in the library. He saw Philip's own wild mad eyes.

'Philip doesn't think this is harmless,' he said.

'No,' said the abbot gravely. 'He doesn't. In fact, it's given him a terrible shock.'

'He was very disturbed anyway. He told you about the body?'

'Yes. A mystery, certainly, but there are a lot of mysteries lately. I see no need to drag in the supernatural.'

The abbot said the word with some distaste. Then he sighed.

'Philip told me once, jokingly I thought, that if you scratch an Irishman you'll find a superstitious peasant under his skin. They have a *doppelgänger* legend here too, you know. It's called a fetch. It's a messenger of death – a messenger from hell, some say.'

Ordinarily that might have sounded funny. It didn't sound very funny now.

'Who *is* Philip?' Stephen asked.

'What do you mean?'

'He has guns – handguns. He handles them like he knows what he's doing. And he shoots people without hesitating. Who *is* he?'

The abbot pursed his lips. He sighed.

'Philip confessed to me yesterday,' he said, 'that he was very tempted to kill you in the library.'

'I guessed that. I could see it in his face. I'm surprised he didn't.'

Paul nodded. He stopped for a while, collecting his thoughts.

'I suppose I may tell you about him,' he said. 'It might help you to understand the pressure he lives under at the best of times. I won't try to excuse him, but a man is what he is not what he was.'

That's easy for you to say, Stephen thought – you know

what you've been and what you are. I've just found out that I may be a messenger from hell. But he said nothing, and the abbot told him Philip's story.

16. The Special Case

'Brother Philip,' the abbot began, 'is the only Irish monk here. The basic purpose of this abbey is to train novices, and our order prefers to train its novices in countries other than their own. Philip came to our doors about ten years ago, shortly after we first arrived here. He asked to join the order. For various reasons, not least his age, it would have been unusual for him to be posted here in Ireland, even if he was accepted. But after he told me his story I arranged for him to join, and pulled some strings so that he could stay with us for his novitiate and afterwards. I might have done better to send him away, I don't know. But he was a special case.'

He paused. He was a man careful with words. He preferred to take his time, to find exactly the right expression.

'Philip,' he said, 'was a terrorist – over across the border there. I use the word 'terrorist' as neutrally as I can. One man's terrorist is another man's freedom-fighter. In my experience their methods tend to be identical – a freedom-fighter is what history calls a terrorist who succeeds. I don't presume to judge others. I try not to have opinions on things which are none of my business. I fail, of course, but when I do have opinions on such things I keep them to myself.'

He was watching Stephen carefully as he spoke, as though for a reaction to the news of Philip's past. But Stephen just thought that at least now he understood Philip's familiarity with guns.

'Philip was never a bomber,' Paul went on. 'He was a specialist, a marksman. But many of his friends dealt with explosives. One day, one of these friends asked Philip to do him a favour – to store some explosives in his house for a day. At the time Philip lived with his parents and his younger sister, whom he especially adored. He didn't want to endanger or incriminate them by keeping explosives in their house, but it was an emergency. His friend was holding the explosives for a bombing team that was due to plant them that night. He'd received a tip-off that his own hiding-place was known, and that he himself was to be arrested that day. In the circumstances, Philip decided to take the risk. His family fully supported him in his activities. Far from condemning his involvement, they were proud of him. But Philip didn't tell them about the explosives, because he didn't want to worry them.

'Philip was working all night that night – at his legitimate job, I mean. He warned his family that someone would be calling late to collect something from their house. There had been other such occasions, although never involving material such as this. But Philip's family trusted him implicitly and never asked questions. At such times they went to their beds early and listened to the quiet footsteps downstairs in the middle of the night without going down. The idea was that they could never be forced to identify anybody they had never seen. This of course is not so, as anyone who's had dealings with an army fighting terrorism will tell you – one can be made to do all sorts of impossible things. But anyway, Philip gave the spare key of his parents' house to the leader of the bombing team and told him exactly where he had hidden the material.'

He paused again, and looked down at his feet.

'Something went wrong,' he said quietly. 'Perhaps all the moving around had made the explosives unstable – there's no way of knowing now. At any rate, the material detonated when the bombers tried to move it. Everyone in the house was killed, both the bombers and the sleeping family. Four people in the adjoining houses – including two small children – were also killed, and several maimed.'

He stopped speaking. There was silence for a while.

'And Philip did … what?' Stephen asked.

'He left the world. He felt he'd killed his family. At first he meant to kill himself. Then he turned to alcohol, which is only a slower way of doing the same thing. Then he left his city and crossed the border, living rough in the mountains for a time. And then he came to us. How he'd heard of us I don't know. I took him in. He's been an excellent Brother, especially popular with the novices. He still supports the cause he fought for then, a little at least. No man would be happier to see peace in that poor place, I think. But it's only his own involvement that he's terminated. He's still indirectly involved at times, I regret to say. We're very close to the border here. I've known for a long time that Philip occasionally holds things for people: packages, letters, small pieces of equipment. No explosives, of course – Philip won't have anything to do with explosives again. But certainly other things.'

'Such as pistols,' Stephen said.

'I hadn't known, but obviously yes.'

'And you never interfered?'

'No. I could stop what he does, but that wouldn't change his mind. Instead I waited for him to see sense. That's what our order does: it encourages, it doesn't demand. We don't believe ideals can be enforced by mere physical might any more than they can be suppressed by it. So long as he didn't endanger his fellow monks it seemed a matter for Philip alone. And I knew that he'd never endanger the monks – the order is like a second family to him. The novices all look up to him, and he takes that responsibility seriously. I may have been wrong not to interfere, but do remember that if Philip hadn't been armed either you or Fräulein Herzenweg might be dead.'

Stephen didn't know what to say. The abbot looked at him with sympathy.

'Will you do something for me, Stephen?' he asked.

'Of course.'

'We've said nothing to Fräulein Herzenweg about what happened in the town. She knows something is wrong, but not what it is. I wanted to talk to you first. She's extremely upset.'

'She would be. So am I.'

'I wondered whether you could tell her about the doubles? She must be told. You're a similar age, and it may be easier for her to hear these things from … a fellow sufferer.'

Stephen nodded.

'Of course,' he said. 'Of course I'll tell her, if I can think how.'

'Thank you,' the abbot said. 'She's been waiting to see you. She was asleep in a chair the last time I saw her. I'll send her up. And about these … *manifestations*. They're certainly strange, but we've no reason to think that they're harmful. Do try to remember that the one yesterday seems deliberately to have saved your lives.'

Damn your fairness, Stephen thought, it's not you these things are happening to. But of course he didn't say that.

'Yes,' he said instead. 'Yes, I know.'

And he did know it too. But he drew no comfort from the knowledge.

The abbot left. Stephen lay back in his bed. The thought struck him suddenly that for all he knew his double might be appearing to someone at that very moment. It gave him an odd feeling. He felt the flesh creep on his bruised and weary bones, and he was very afraid.

17. The Desperate Girl

It was a while before Kirsten came to see him. When she did come she brought a pot of coffee on the now familiar tray. She was obviously upset, though she tried to hide it under a veneer of mock gaiety. But the tell-tale redness was around her eyes.

'I think we should start charging you for room service,' she said.

There were two cups on the tray. Stephen's nostrils flared at the scent of fresh coffee.

'I didn't know whether or not to bring food,' Kirsten said.

'The coffee smells good, but I'm not hungry.'

He watched her as she poured coffee into the cups. She was pale and tired-looking, her slim shoulders slumped, but she was ... *solid*. She was solid, and so was he. There was nothing ghostly about them. And only ghosts and saints and devils, so far as he'd heard, could be in two places at the same time, and he couldn't believe that either of them was any of those things.

Looking at her scared face, he wondered how he was going to get up the nerve to tell her what had happened. He'd agreed to the abbot's request without thinking. Now he baulked at the idea of causing her more upset than she'd already endured.

'We were very lucky yesterday,' he said.

'Yes. But I keep thinking, you know ... I *killed* someone.'

Stephen hadn't even thought of the effect of that on her.

'He was trying to kill you,' he pointed out.

'I know. But that doesn't make it feel any better. I know it sounds stupid, but ... that was *his* business. As it happened, I killed him. I didn't mean to, but still I did and that's *my* business.'

'Philip killed three of them. He didn't seem too disturbed.'

'I don't know about that. I wanted to talk to Philip about it, I thought maybe he'd tell me something that would help me feel better. But he shunned me. He wouldn't even look at me. And you know, Philip has been so nice to me since I came here. I really like him ... liked him. But now ...'

She waved her hands in a helpless sort of gesture. Her eyes gleamed in the dim light and Stephen had a sudden, terrible feeling that she was going to cry again. He felt flustered.

'Philip saved our lives,' he said quickly. 'I'm sure of that.'

'I know, I know.'

Stephen felt sorry for her. She'd been so determined to make the best of things. From their first meeting she'd seemed almost relieved by the loss of her past. She'd been born again, flung into a new world full of possibilities. She'd borne up more bravely than he had to a whole series of shocks. Now her cheerful façade had collapsed like a house of cards.

'It will be all right,' he lied. 'We didn't know how dangerous it could be out there. Next time we'll be better prepared.'

He knew he was getting no closer to telling her what he'd promised to tell. But how exactly did you go about telling someone something like that? He doubted he'd ever had any experience of such things in his forgotten life.

Kirsten needed to talk about what had happened in the town, and he let her. As she talked, he understood just how upset she was. She was appalled by the fact that she'd killed someone, whatever the circumstances. She'd got along well with Philip, and she'd hoped for reassurance if not comfort from him. Instead she'd met with something that upset her far more than hostility.

'After you passed out,' she said, 'Philip wanted to leave the library right away. We even abandoned those stupid books we were collecting. We had to carry you to the truck, but Philip seemed reluctant to even touch you. If I hadn't badgered him I think he'd have left you there. In the end he carried you, though he obviously didn't like it. He put you in the back of the truck, and I went with you. The trip back was a *nightmare*. Philip drove so recklessly I thought we'd crash, and you were sliding all over the place. I had to keep your head from banging into the sides of the truck-bed, and then I was sliding around too on the corners.'

She was getting upset just talking about it. Her shoulders were clenched tight and her fists were clenched too, the knuckles white.

'When we got back,' she said, 'Philip went off and just left us there. I sat in the back of the truck with your head in my lap and just cried. Simon came to help us in the end. He doesn't approve of Philip, and he was making all sorts of snide remarks about peasant superstitions. Eventually we got you up here and I went to corner Philip. I found him coming out of the abbot's office. He was very gruff. He wouldn't meet my eyes at all. But I did see his, just for a second, and I couldn't believe what I saw in them. It was—'

'Fear,' Stephen said. 'You saw fear in them.'

Kirsten stared at him.

'Yes. But more than that — it was fear of *me*. And I thought ...'

Again she gestured helplessly.

'I don't know what I thought,' she said.

'Have you spoken with the abbot?'

'He's talked to me, yes. And Simon has. They tried to reassure me, and they were very kind. Simon even told me that he's killed people himself, during the war. But I still feel ... I feel like a *murderer*. Maybe that's why Philip is afraid of me.'

'It's got nothing to do with that.'

'No? What does it have to do with then? Why are we suddenly so terrifying?'

Stephen thought of Philip in the field, his wild eyes searching for the vanished body. What had the big monk said then: *What devil's work is this?* Then he looked at Kirsten, so obviously human. He was going mad himself even to consider such nonsense.

'You know something I don't,' Kirsten said angrily. 'Don't you? You know why Philip is afraid.'

Stephen hung his head. He suddenly resented Paul's request. He felt he'd been given the job of destroying her altogether.

'I–' he began.

But he got no further. From outside the drawn curtains there was a sudden babble of voices, but Stephen couldn't make out what they were saying. Had someone else wandered in? Or was it an attack by another group of savages?

Then, over the babble, Stephen and Kirsten could hear another sound.

'That sounds like …' Kirsten began. Her voice trailed off.

'It *is*!' Stephen said.

They ran for the window and snatched back the curtains. It had grown fully light as they talked. Philip came into view, the big pistol in his hand. His face was grim. Behind him came the abbot, empty-handed. They stood in front of the well, staring towards the gateway.

'Open the gates!' Philip called in a choked voice.

'Oh Lord,' Kirsten said a moment later.

The sound they'd heard was exactly what it sounded like: a car engine. The car drew up in front of Philip and the abbot. Old Brother Simon and Thomas, the novice, came up behind it. Simon held a shotgun; Thomas held what looked like Philip's little silver pistol. Both aimed their guns squarely at the car. Philip still kept the big automatic hanging limply by his side. His face was white, and devoid of any expression whatsoever.

The babble of voices had yielded to complete silence.

Beside him, Stephen heard Kirsten moan a low moan, a whimpering animal sound of pure undiluted terror. He knew the source of that terror, because it was the source of his own – they'd seen the car's occupants.

There were three men in the car. In the back sat a stout dark-haired man who looked annoyed. In the front were two slim men in dark suits. One, the driver, was a dour-faced man in a grey hat. He looked to be maybe in his late forties. But it was the third man who inspired terror – the man in the front passenger seat. He was sitting casually, with his torso turned towards the driver, one arm resting on the back of his seat and the other fiddling idly with his tie. Stephen couldn't say what this man looked like, and he couldn't say what the man looked like for the same reason that the man inspired such terror. The man in the front seat had no head.

PART TWO: The Big Bubble

18. Monday

Let's skip back in time a few days and look at all this from another angle. Let's take a peek at the bigger picture.

Early one Monday morning in Ireland, a man and a woman woke up in a car. They found they were parked in the middle of a field, and that the car was surrounded by sheep.

The man and the woman were confused. They didn't recall driving into a field and going asleep. In fact, they didn't remember going to sleep at all. The last thing they remembered was going home from a dinner-dance late the night before, driving down the dark country roads, longing to be home. And they remembered that – or at least they *thought* they remembered that – quite clearly.

When they got out of the car to look around they were even more puzzled. The field they were in was low-lying and boggy so that the ground was wet even after the fine summer weather. The earth was so soft that even the sheep left hoof-prints in it. Yet there were no tyre-tracks behind the car, no sign that they'd ever actually driven there at all. It was as though the vehicle had been plucked up by a giant hand and then gently deposited here where it was now parked.

The other strange thing was that they couldn't see any

mountains. They'd been driving in their own part of the country where the mountains were always visible on the horizon at least. Yet here there were none to be seen.

The man and the woman also noticed that their watches had stopped, and stopped at precisely the same time: 3.57am.

The woman grew frightened. The man grew frightened too, but didn't want the woman to see this. So he tried to look tough. He stared up at the sky, where there was nothing much to see beyond an old crow flapping lazily on its way to nowhere in particular, which must be a special place for crows because they always look as though they're going there.

'I've seen this kind of thing before,' the man said.

This came as a surprise to the woman – he'd never struck her as a man who'd had a single odd thing happen to him in his whole life. But it turned out that he meant he'd seen it on television.

'Mary,' the man said gravely, 'I suspect we were abducted by a You Eff Oh.'

'Lord save us!' the woman said, and shivered.

Quite a number of people were having odd awakenings that Monday morning, and all of their experiences had several things in common. Firstly, they woke up in places that they knew full well they hadn't gone to sleep in. Secondly, they were miles from their homes. Thirdly, when they did wake they found themselves dressed in whatever they'd been wearing at about four o'clock that morning: nightclothes, mainly. And fourthly and finally, not one of them could remember a single thing about how they'd got to where they were. They were found wandering the roads by early-morning travellers, or blundered dazed into half-awake villages and towns, or turned up, scared and bleary-eyed, in the yards of scattered farmhouses. They woke in fields and on top of haystacks. They woke in town squares or parks. They woke – someone soon noticed – in reasonably *safe* places, away from roads, where nothing dangerous would be likely to happen to them while they slept. It was as though someone had deliberately *placed* them. It was all extremely *spooky*, and it got spookier the more you thought about it.

Gradually, as dawn became morning and the country of Ireland woke up, word spread that something very strange had taken place in one of its less populated areas. At the very least a great epidemic of sleepwalking (and in a couple of cases the even stranger sleep*driving*) seemed to have broken out. And as the reports of the sufferers became better known, an even weirder fact became clear: whatever had happened, it had happened in a relatively small area around the mountains to the northwest. Every one of the sufferers either lived in that area or had been passing through it at 4am that morning, when the strange thing – whatever it was – seemed to have taken place.

It soon became clear that in the middle of the previous night, in a corner of Ireland, while nobody was looking, something terribly, terribly odd had taken place. Someone, or something, had evicted all the people. Nobody knew why or how, least of all those who'd been evicted. And naturally everyone was puzzled, because it's not the sort of thing that happens every day.

Naturally too, the police were interested immediately. Everybody was. The first reporters arrived in the area within the hour. Strange and garbled and downright foolish reports were broadcast from the northwest itself – because, of course, it hadn't taken long before people began to wonder what exactly was going on up there, and a few hardy souls had gone to take a look. And soon the rumours flew, and grew as they flew, as rumours will. And then the soldiers started coming, and the helicopters, and by noon the first of the international television crews. Cool-headed shopkeepers in villages close to the centre of events – those villages which still had anyone in them – began to take a longer view of things, and rubbed their hands, and raised their prices, and sat back to wait and watch.

19. Reputation One

At first the spectators saw only movement, a seething mass of ... what? Earth? Water? No. Something alive. Some kind of insect? Ants? A beehive in enormous close-up?

Suddenly the camera zoomed in and the scene on the screen became clearer. There were gasps in the dark room as it became obvious that what they were seeing was a crowd of human beings. But such a crowd! Such a mass of pushing, shoving, clawing humanity! The camera, panning, showed no end to it.

The watchers could make out no details, only the struggling masses. Then the camera zoomed in again, still panning here and there, and they could spot individual areas of the crowd. Here was a large group, led by a figure in black, carrying banners with religious pictures on them. In fact, there were many such religious groups, some of them kneeling, obviously praying, while the crowd surged around them. A knot of orange-robed Krishna devotees banged drums and shook rattles and tambourines as they moved along. There was a tight group of what looked like film cameramen carrying big professional-looking video cameras on their shoulders. There were many different groups, but most of the great crowd seemed made up of individuals. And all of them, whether singly or in groups, were struggling in the same direction: forward.

'The numbers have been growing from day one,' said a voice in the darkness. 'A trickle of sightseers began as soon as the first news reports were released. That trickle very quickly became a flood, as you can see. The pictures you see here were taken at eleven o'clock last night. The best available estimates put the numbers on the screen at something between fifteen and twenty thousand people. Thousands more will have arrived since then by every available means of transport. They're coming from all over the world, and our port and air-port facilities are already stretched to full capacity. They've never seen anything like this: that's the problem – no one has.'

The speaker's voice quivered on the final phrase. He cleared his throat.

'There are gatherings this large or larger,' he said, 'at approximately twenty places along the perimeter. There are smaller crowds at an estimated sixteen further locations. All in all we estimate that as of noon today, there were well over half a million people gathered around The Phenomenon.'

The images had been filmed from a helicopter. Now the chopper swirled up and away from the crowd itself, the camera panning again to show the scene behind. Great banks of searchlights shone blinding beams of light, illuminating a gigantic campsite of caravans, marquees and tents, of all sorts of rickety shelters and thousands of sleeping bags thrown on the bare ground. Beside the campsite stood row upon row of mobile chip vans, and a great nomad city of stalls offering everything from fast food to holy relics to tarot card readings.

'These scenes were filmed at a place called Doulapown,' the voice said. 'Until two days ago it had a permanent population of exactly zero and a part-time population composed largely of migratory birds. It now has a tourist information office, seventeen churches and temples based in tents and marquees, twenty illegal bars, two *bureaux de change* and a bank.'

Another voice came from the group of shadows sitting in the darkness. 'What about crowd control?'

'Watch.'

The camera panned again, to the front of the crowd this time. You could see that the whole mass was fringed by a thin line of police and soldiers who were struggling to hold it back. They were on a fool's errand. It was hard to gauge how many of them there were, but compared to the numbers surging forward they were too few to offer more than token resistance. Slowly but surely they were being pushed back.

'A good rainstorm would do more to clear the area than we can,' the first voice said. 'The army and police presence at Doulapown is higher than at any other location on the perimeter. But as you can see, it's completely ineffective. We have only so many soldiers and policemen, and they do have other duties. Secondment of police from the cities and the larger towns has already led to crime-levels in these reaching crisis point.'

'What about water-cannon?' the second voice asked. 'Tear gas? There are methods, you know.'

This voice was brusque, clipped, American. Several throats were cleared uncomfortably at its words.

'We're aware that there are methods,' the first voice replied. 'We're just not entirely comfortable with the idea of using them. Not with publicity being the way it is. You must realise that the Phenomenon is the lead story on every news bulletin on earth right now. Media people in the area probably out-number clergy.'

'But you can't–' began the American voice. Then, in mid-sentence, it broke into a gasp. The sound was lost in the simultaneous chorus of gasps that broke out in the darkness. Even the Irish government representatives present had trouble containing themselves, though they'd seen the thing before – had been watching pictures of it for two whole days. Some had seen it with their own eyes, and that was even more impressive. The others must have seen pictures of it too, of course, but early shots hadn't conveyed its sheer...*otherness*.

The camera had continued its pan, past the crowd and past the soldiers. It had come to rest on The Phenomenon itself: vast, beautiful, inexplicable, terrifying, mystifying – and yet, to the eye at least, looking so fragile as to be hardly there.

Ahead of the crowd, lit by the banks of searchlights and the last light of the dying summer sun, an enormous wall of vaguely iridescent purple haze rose from the ground. It went up and up, its summit hidden in clouds. At ground level the haze stretched as far as the eye could see. It was indisputably there, and yet it looked no more substantial than a soap-bubble. It looked like a weather phenomenon, a bizarre trick of the light.

'Gentlemen,' said the first voice, which belonged to the Irish Minister for Defence. 'May I introduce to you the reason for this meeting – the Bubble, the Barrier, the Purple Haze, call it what you will. The popular press are having competitions to find a name – the front-runner at the moment seems to be The Ball that's a Wall.'

He paused, as though waiting for a laugh. None came.

'For our purposes,' the Minister said, 'its name is The Phenomenon. Its official code-name is Reputation One.'

All eyes lingered on the impossible sight on the screen. The Phenomenon was translucent. Beyond the wall of purple could be seen the empty fields of a completely ordinary Irish countryside.

'Sightings of animal life beyond the wall of The Phenomenon are common,' the Minister said. 'The animals show no signs of unease. That means things inside are at least reasonably normal – there's air and so on.'

'Any sightings of humans in there, or … you know… anything *else*?'

'None that we know of.'

'Have all the inhabitants of the area been accounted for?'

'The, um, vast majority of them, yes.'

'But not all?'

'No. There's … an *abbey* in the mountains there. It's run by a rather peculiar order of monks based in Switzerland.'

'*Monks?*'

'Monks. We've contacted their headquarters in Berne. They say there should be four monks there in the abbey: a Swiss, a Belgian, an Irishman and a young Frenchman. Noone answering their descriptions has turned up among the displaced persons.'

'You've tried phoning the abbey, I presume?' someone asked.

The Irish Minister sighed patiently.

'Yes, we have,' he said. 'There was no sound on the line at all. Nothing. There's no sound on any line leading inside that area. No phonecalls can go in there, no radio signals can go in there, no people can go in there, no vehicles can go in there. To judge from the lack of any artificial light at night-time from anywhere inside, even electricity can't go in. *Nothing* can go in!'

He looked again to where their eyes were all still fixed – the softly glowing haze on the screen. In the darkness he raised his arm and pointed a slightly shaky finger at the image.

'Gentlemen,' he said, his voice quivering, 'someone or something has emptied a part of my country of its people, and put that *thing* there to stop them from returning to their homes. We don't know who's done it, and we don't know why. What we do know is that for several days now a part of Ireland has been seized and occupied, every bit as much as if a foreign army had landed. My country has been invaded, gentlemen, and we've asked you here because we badly need your advice.'

20. The Appliance of Science

The lights came up in the conference room, and the big screen went blank. The men – they were all men – sat with strained faces and looked at the podium beside the screen where the Minister for Defence stood leafing through a sheaf of papers in a file. They'd seen how close he'd come to losing control, but none of them thought any the worse of him for it. They imagined how they'd feel if this had happened in their own countries; then they imagined how much worse they'd feel if they were the person supposed to make sure that things like this didn't happen.

'We've been studying Reputation One almost since it first appeared,' the Minister said. 'A team of government scientists and engineers was sent to the area as soon as we realised the extent of the problem.'

The scientists hadn't, he admitted, discovered much by way of useful information. They could see from both air and ground observation that the Phenomenon – visually at least – resembled nothing so much as a gigantic soap-bubble composed of a sort of purple mist. Tests made from helicopters suggested that its notable characteristics aloft were exactly the same as at ground level. As above, so below. Exploratory tunnelling at several sites seemed to confirm that these characteristics continued underground. The Phenomenon might very well be spherical, with only half of it visible above ground. And even that half was extremely impressive, effectively barring humanity from some three hundred square kilometres of the island of Ireland. As to what it was *made* of, nobody could determine. The haze might or might not be made of a material unknown to science, but the scientists couldn't analyse it because they couldn't obtain a sample.

'You've tried using lasers?' someone asked.

'Of course we have! The beam simply bounced off – and came close to slicing our top scientist in half. Naturally he was in no hurry to repeat the experiment. We've also tried to penetrate the barrier using artillery.'

'And?'

'And it doesn't work. *Nothing* works. The odd thing is that the haze is in no way hard or shell-like to the touch – I've touched it myself. It feel at first rather like dipping your hand into tepid water. But after that resistance grows very quickly. The deepest we've managed to penetrate so far is six centimetres. It should be noted too that only living or once-living organic material will penetrate the haze at all.'

They all looked queries at him.

'A piece of dead wood, or a human limb, or even a bit of grass,' the Minister said, 'will penetrate further and more easily than a blade or a bullet – or an artillery shell.'

There was general muttering from his audience.

'Our people have tried various on-site tests on the

substance,' the Minister went on. He sounded vaguely bitter. 'Tests for chemical reactions and so on. Results ranged from the completely useless to the worse-than-useless. In fact, several reliable chemical tests strongly suggest that the Phenomenon isn't actually there at all.'

Eyes strayed to the now-blank screen. None of them could forget the impact of that first real sight of the Bubble. It was there all right.

Generally speaking, the Minister went on, scientific investigation told them only three things, none very helpful. First, no one could say what Reputation One was made of. Second, they didn't know who, or what, had put it there. Third, they didn't know *why* they'd put it there. Which basically meant they were no better off than they'd been two days ago when the thing first appeared. In short, the Irish government's best scientific brains were baffled. Meanwhile, in the space of those two days the thing had become the biggest tourist attraction on the face of the planet. It had become a site of pilgrimage for half the religions in the world, and for all anyone knew it could at any moment grow, shrink, explode, or open up to release who knew what mayhem on the surrounding crowds, not to mention the rest of humankind.

The Minister's voice had been growing shakier again as he spoke. By now he sounded almost tearful. He stopped and took control of himself again. He cleared his throat and fiddled with his tie. Then he filled a glass of water from a carafe beside him on the podium and drank it.

'Yesterday,' he said, 'we sent out a call to all friendly

governments. Your presence here is the result of that appeal. This problem is located in Ireland, but it's not simply an Irish problem. This thing may be the first of many, or it may contain something that will prove in time to be a danger to us all. The Phenomenon may represent a threat to all of humanity.'

He filled and gulped down another glass of water.

'Gentlemen,' he said, 'I come here today with a very simple but extremely heartfelt message from the Irish government and the Irish people, and the gist of that message is this: *Help!*'

21. Developments

The conference was being held in a network of underground rooms and bunkers lying below Government Buildings in Dublin. It was being held in secret, and was perhaps the only place in the whole country not overrun by film-crews. There were plenty of reporters and cameramen outside Government Buildings, of course, waiting to ask emerging politicians for the latest news. But the real news was happening, as it so often does, in quiet air-conditioned rooms underground, where middle-aged well-groomed men in expensive suits (guarded by squads of cold-eyed, younger, well-groomed men wearing ear-pieces, shiny shoes and a variety of government-issue sidearms) discussed the appropriate response to the Big Bubble.

The conference continued in non-stop session. Various delegates, exhausted, would go for a rest in the small but comfortable bedrooms provided. Often they'd sleep, and when they slept they often dreamed of Reputation One. Some even had nightmares about it. Later, rested, they'd return. Food would be brought in at regular intervals by some of the cold-eyed young men. The talk never stopped. They talked hot air, but then politicians are used to that. They even find a kind of comfort in it: it makes them feel they're doing something. The number of people arriving into the country grew, and the army and police at the site of the Bubble lost even more control. But at the conference, attended by experts on everything, who'd come from everywhere, nothing changed. Until around midday on Saturday. When everything did.

By Saturday morning the scenes around the perimeter of The Phenomenon had gone well beyond the point where they could be described as chaotic. The word 'chaos' no longer did them justice. By now almost three million people surrounded the baseof the Big Bubble. The police and army had abandoned all serious efforts at crowd-control. They'd been reduced to firing volleys in the air over people's heads, and even these were gradually growing less effective as a deterrent.

The camp at Doulapown had by now grown into a shanty-city with an estimated eighty-five thousand residents. The number of churches and temples had grown to twenty-eight, the number of illegal bars to a hundred and seventy-five. The Big Bubble frenzy had not died – it had intensified intensely.

Just before midday the main conference room under Government Buildings in Dublin was completely silent. It was the first time it had been so quiet since the initial meeting on Tuesday. The silence, brief but deep, had been caused by the senior United States security representative, General Tubb. The general, frustrated by four days of failure to penetrate the barrier at all, had made what he considered a very practical suggestion. From the silence, the white faces and the way everyone else stared goggle-eyed at him, he suspected that not everyone shared his opinion.

'I didn't mean a *big* nuclear bomb,' he hastened to reassure them. 'I only meant a teensie one. We drop it right on top of that old bubble' – he demonstrated with his cigar – 'and BOOM! – no more bubble. It might just work, and I happened to bring one over on the plane with me that would be *just* the right size. I never go anywhere without one – you never know when it might come in handy.'

The explanation didn't seem to please anyone at all. Finally the Irish Minister for Defence, who looked more than drained after four days of intense pressure, dragged himself to his feet.

'General, we've proven,' he said, speaking quite slowly, as one might to a small child, 'that things bounce *off* The Phenomenon. Throw something at the haze, it rebounds at almost exactly twice the speed. That's one of the few definite facts about it that we've managed to establish.'

'So?'

'So, General, what if your bomb doesn't explode? What if it rebounds and lands on Belfast or Galway?' He pointed directly overhead. 'General, what if it drops right here on Dublin?'

General Tubb looked puzzled. He glanced narrowly at the ceiling. 'You mean this place isn't nuke-proof?' he asked suspiciously.

There was a knock at the door. There was something odd about the knock. The cold-eyed young men always knocked before entering, but even their knocks were cold-eyed: a steely, professional *Rat-Tat* that they all seemed to use, as though they'd all learned it at the same school. This knock was different. It consisted of five raps in a rhythm some of the room's occupants would have called *shave-and-a-haircut*. It sounded almost cheerful.

The conference delegates looked at each other.

'Come in,' called the Minister for Defence.

The door swung open and an unlikely figure peered in at them apologetically. It was a fat little old woman with blue-rinsed hair. A pale pink cardigan hung around her shoulders. Horn-rimmed glasses hung on a chain around her neck. Her hands were empty, held out palms upwards.

'I'm sorry to bother you,' she said. 'But I thought you'd like to know that you can stop worrying now. We've almost finished what we came to do, and our exclusion zone will be removed before midnight.'

At first no one heard what she said. Seeing her there was so unlikely that the delegates hardly even noticed her. Instead they all looked past her, to where a pile of cold-eyed well-groomed young men wearing ear-pieces and shiny shoes lay, neatly and rigidly, stacked like so much firewood against the corridor wall behind her. They all looked very dead.

22 · The Little Fat Woman

The little fat woman smiled at the conference delegates. Then she noticed where their attention was directed. She glanced back at the neat stack of cold-eyed young men.

'Oh, your guards!' she said. 'I'm sorry. But they didn't want me to come in. They'll be fine later, and they'll remember none of this.'

Now the delegates' eyes did swivel in her direction. They stared at her blankly. There had been twenty highly-trained security men in the corridor. This little woman looked incapable of disabling anything more fearsome than a reasonably well-built plastic bag. Still, the security men lay there, and the little fat woman said she'd done it, and she wasn't even out of breath.

The little fat woman seemed to read their minds. She smiled cheerfully.

'You mustn't be taken in by my appearance,' she said. 'I'm what you might call a master of disguise.'

And she gave a little giggle, as though at some private joke.

The delegates' eyes followed the little fat woman as she walked up the room to the podium, where the Irish Minister for Defence stood with his mouth slightly open. As the woman reached the top of the room, General Tubb suddenly rose and blocked her way. He stood glaring down at the little fat woman.

'Say,' he said, 'what's the meaning of this?'

The little woman looked directly up into the General's blue eyes. She seemed to read some message there.

'Dearie me,' she said. 'I can see there'll be no use in talking to *you*.'

She made a delicate little gesture with one hand. General Tubb sat down hard on the floor and stayed there, perfectly still. The little fat woman stepped around him. The delegates closest to the general stared at his sitting form. One of them waved a hand close to the General's face. He didn't blink. Another reached out a nervous hand and prodded at the General with his finger. The General tottered, overbalanced and fell on his back. His body didn't bend. His legs stuck straight up in the air. The delegates stared in disbelief.

The little fat woman reached the podium.

'You may as well sit down,' she said kindly to the Minister for Defence.

The Minister for Defence nodded.

'I suppose I may as well,' he said. He sounded dazed.

The little fat woman looked around the room. Every eye was fixed on her. She nodded.

'Gentlemen,' she said, 'my business here is simple. I've already told you what I came to say. Your worries are over. We will be removing our barrier – what you call The Phenomenon – very shortly. We would like to apologise for the inconvenience. Believe me, we'd much rather none of this had happened. If we had any other way of dealing with the situation then I assure you we would have done so.'

Someone among the delegates found their voice. It was a fairly strangled voice, but it was clear enough.

'Wh-what situation?' it asked.

'I'm afraid I'm not at liberty to say.'

Encouraged, someone else piped up.

'You say "we". Who are "we"? Who *are* you?'

A frosty little smile touched the woman's lips.

'Me? Why, I'm no one in particular. As regards "we", well …'

She hesitated.

'Don't tell me,' said the Minister for Defence, 'you're not at liberty to say, right?'

'It would take a long time,' said the little fat woman. 'A very long time. And you might be happier not knowing.'

'But I *want* to know!' the Minister said, his voice rising a few octaves. 'Whoever you are, you can't just hive off part of my country, cause an international panic, then simply turn up and say it's all over and you're sorry for the inconvenience!'

The little fat woman smiled at him coyly. Her eyes positively twinkled.

'I can, you know,' she said.

She turned and, selecting a spot on the wall right behind her, walked right through it and was gone. In her wake the conference room degenerated into bedlam. Which, admittedly, it had never been very far from anyway.

PART THREE: The Fix-It Men

23. The Dead Coach

'I want this to stop,' Kirsten said.

'It's not going to stop,' Stephen said, trying to sound calmer than he felt. 'All we can do now is see it through to the end.'

'I don't want to know what the end is. I want it all to go away *now*.'

Stephen stared at the scene outside. The monks were moving back slowly, recoiling as the reality of what they were seeing sank in.

'I want to run away and hide too,' he said. 'But there's nowhere to go.'

'Then I just want to curl up and die,' Kirsten said.

He looked at her. Her eyes were wide, registering something way beyond horror.

'I'm going out there,' he said.

'You're mad!' she whispered.

He shook his head.

'They need all the support they can get,' he said firmly. 'And I doubt there's one of them out there less terrified than we are.'

But Kirsten was already backing away from the window, one hand thrown up in front of her face as though to protect her from the sight of the scene outside. She was shaking her head.

'Don't,' she said. 'Please, don't go out.'

But he was already going, forcing himself put one foot in front of the other.

As he went down the stairs he heard feet running, and when he got outside he saw that the scene there had changed. Thomas's nerve had finally cracked, and he was running in panic across the courtyard towards the doorway of the bell-tower. The little pistol lay on the ground where he'd dropped it. The three monks remaining stood facing the car. Philip, his right hand shaking visibly, held his pistol up in front of him, aiming it at the driver, who opened the door and casually got out. Stephen crossed to stand beside the abbot, keeping his eyes on the driver, unwilling to look at the headless passenger in the front seat.

The man who got out of the car was small and slight. He brushed down his suit and straightened his tie. The thin face under the dark hat was smooth and reserved, and his pale eyes looked at them shrewdly as he stood away from the car. His hands, hanging at his sides, were empty. He held them out, palms up, as though in token of peaceful intent.

'Good morning,' he said pleasantly in a clear voice. He took his hat off and held it in front of him. The morning sun shone on his thinning sandy hair. He looked terribly ordinary. It was hard to believe he could be a party to such terror.

Nobody answered his greeting. He looked around thought-fully at their tense faces. The three monks stood like statues, apart from Philip's quivering hand. Simon's face was every bit as impassive as the driver's. He held his gun trained on the car, steady as a rock.

The driver completed his survey of their faces. His eyes turned to Philip. He nodded at the black pistol wavering in the big man's hand.

'Be careful with that,' he said mildly. 'You might blow a hole in something.'

'In you, maybe,' Philip said. The bravado of his words rang hollow. The driver smiled a smile that was actually quite pleasant.

'Very possibly,' he said. 'And that would be inconvenient. I have work to do, and I can't do without a body just yet.'

He spoke with no suggestion of threat. It was only his words that sounded crazy.

'Who are you people, and what do you want?' demanded the abbot.

The man looked at him, still smiling.

'I'll be happy to satisfy your curiosity,' he said. 'But right now I was hoping that you could lend some unfortunate travellers some assistance. As you can see, we've had a little accident.'

He gestured with his hat towards the interior of the car. *A little accident!* There was something almost brutal about the phrase when you considered what he was obviously referring to.

'I wonder,' the man said, 'whether you'd have a quiet place where my friend could rest for a little while. Just a small time, to recuperate. After that I'll be only too pleased to answer any questions you have.'

His demeanour made the whole situation seem quite unreal. His words didn't help. In the real world people don't 'recuperate' after being beheaded.

The abbot was having trouble keeping control of himself. You could hear it in his voice. But the stranger's request had at least put the situation into some kind of familiar context.

'Forgive my manners,' he said. 'You must realise that your appearance is … unusual, to say the least.'

'Of course. I quite understand. But now – I don't wish to seem hasty, but the sooner I can tend to my friend, the sooner we can sort all this out.'

'God almighty!' Philip's interruption was an angry croak. Looking at his face, Stephen realised that it must have taken all of his willpower not to run away with the novice.

'You're not going to let these … these *things* stay here, are you?' Philip demanded of the abbot.

'I get the impression,' Paul said dryly, 'that I don't have a great deal of choice in the matter.'

He looked at the driver, who shrugged.

'Well,' the man said, 'I don't think any of us have. This is an unfortunate business, but it needs to be sorted out. The sooner it's sorted, the happier I'm certain all of us will be. You can't sort it. We can – it's what we're here for. So sooner or later you'll have to deal with us, and sooner or later we'll have to deal with you. We may as well go about it in a civilised fashion.'

Paul looked at him. Then he nodded.

'Put up your guns,' he said to the other two monks.

Brother Simon obeyed after only a slight hesitation. But Philip's weapon stayed where it was, aimed shakily at the driver's chest. The man looked sniffily at the gun, but when he spoke to Philip his voice was almost apologetic.

'I'm afraid I can't let you kill me,' he said. 'As I've told you, it would be inconvenient.'

'Philip!' Paul said sharply. 'Put it down!'

Philip lowered the pistol reluctantly. His face wasn't so much white as colourless. It shone with a sheen of sweat. His whole body shivered violently.

The abbot spoke quietly to the driver.

'There are bedrooms upstairs, to your left,' he said. 'We'll put your friend in one of them.'

'That would be perfect,' the driver said. He looked into the car, at the thickset man in the back seat.

'Help my friend,' he said curtly. There was nothing mild in his voice now.

The big man got out of the car. He looked around him with distaste. He opened the front passenger door and took the arm of the headless man, who climbed out carefully. Watching him with reluctant fascination, Stephen felt the fear moving in his bowels. They called this thing a man, but it couldn't be a man – headless men are dead men, and this thing wasn't dead. Beside him he heard Philip give a low moan.

The headless man carried a plastic bag in one hand. The

bag was bloody, and it bulged with something solid, something about the size of a human head.

The driver looked around at them.

'It's only an injured body,' he said gently. 'I'm going to fix it, that's all. That's what we're here for, to fix things. We're fix-it men.'

He looked to the abbot, who gestured towards the doorway leading into Stephen's wing of the abbey.

'This way,' he said.

He led the way inside, followed by the driver and then, more slowly, by the thickset man and the headless one. Those in the courtyard stood looking after them, even after they'd disappeared inside. Then the old monk went off towards the bell-tower, looking for the vanished novice. Stephen stood there stupidly, looking around at the car and the abandoned guns lying on the ground. Behind him, Philip said something he didn't catch. He turned around.

'What?' he said.

Philip's eyes had been fixed on the car. When Stephen spoke they turned towards him. Stephen had seen that wild-eyed look more than once now, but never like this. These were truly madman's eyes.

'The dead coach,' Philip said.

The gun in his hand swung up. He held it at the level of his hip, pointed straight at Stephen.

'First the fetch,' Philip said, 'and now the dead coach and its headless rider.'

Stephen remembered what the abbot had said the night

before, that the fetch was his double. What the dead coach or the headless rider might be, he had no idea.

He was terribly aware of the gun in Philip's hand. This was the second time in less than forty-eight hours that the big monk had pointed that gun at him. Yesterday he'd come close to pulling the trigger, but he'd thought better of it; today, to judge by his mad eyes, he wasn't thinking at all.

Stephen licked his lips

'Philip,' he said carefully, 'I swear I know nothing about this. Kirsten and I are as frightened as everyone else.'

Philip stood stiff and unmoving for a moment longer. Stephen could see a sneer forming on his lips.

Then he hit Stephen.

While the boy was watching his face, the monk swung the gun up and hit him in the side of the head with it. It wasn't a heavy blow, but Stephen was stunned, as much by the surprise as by the blow itself. For one moment he thought he'd been shot. He saw stars. When his vision cleared he looked up to see Philip walking away. Stephen stood blinking after him, dazed, his eyes smarting and an ache in his skull. He was suddenly angry. He was a boy; Philip was a man, over six feet tall and built to match. Fear or no fear, he was simply a bully. He wasn't going to do anything like that to Stephen again.

Stephen had already noticed the silver pistol lying on the ground. Now, without thinking, he bent down, scooped it up and stuffed it in his back pocket. Then he heard Kirsten scream.

24. The Friendly Stranger

Stephen raced through the doorway and up the stone stairs. The corridor above was empty when he got there, but the door of the room next to his was ajar. He heard voices inside. He was about to push the door open when the abbot came out. He stopped short when he saw Stephen.

'So,' he said. 'You didn't run away.'

'No. I think I was too frightened. What was that scream? Is Kirsten all right?'

'Yes. She came out of your room as we were passing. She got a bad shock. She almost walked right into the, uh, injured man.'

Stephen looked at the door of his own room. It was firmly shut.

'Can you explain to her?' Paul asked.

Explain? Stephen couldn't even explain it to himself.

'What about you?' he asked. 'Don't you need help?'

'I'm just going to fetch the things that they asked for: towels, water and … a needle and thread.'

'Thread?' said Stephen flatly.

'Yes. Thread. The stronger the better, the man said.'

Stephen thought about that.

'I think I'll talk to Kirsten,' he said.

The abbot nodded, then hurried on his way. Stephen went into his room, careful to knock and call out before he entered.

Kirsten was sitting hunched over by the table, staring glassily at the table top. The very look of her made Stephen pity her. She didn't react when he said her name. He went over and touched her shoulder. When she looked up at him she started to cry silently. The tears ran down her face and she made no effort to wipe them away. Stephen felt unbearably awkward.

'Monstrous!' Kirsten said. 'It's monstrous!'

Her voice shook.

'Please, Kirsten,' Stephen said. 'They say they're here to help. We can't afford to panic. Paul needs us all to be solid now. Thomas lost his … lost control completely. Philip too. There's only us and Simon now.'

She buried her face in her hands and her shoulders shook, but little by little her crying eased. After a while she looked up, trying hard to control her emotions.

'I hate crying,' she said. 'My face puffs up, and I look like a rabbit. I'll be all right, honestly. It was just such a shock walking into that … that *man*.'

There was a polite knock on the door. The abbot, Stephen thought.

'Come in,' he said.

The door opened, and a head looked in. But it wasn't Paul. It was the stranger who'd done the talking in the courtyard – the driver. Once more Stephen was struck by how harmless he looked. Only the shrewdness of his blue eyes suggested anything else. He looked at them now with a pleasant smile.

'Hello,' he said. 'I just wanted to apologise to the young lady for frightening her.'

'Oh,' Stephen said. 'I don't think it was you. Not personally, I mean.'

'No. But it's my responsibility at the moment. I'm pleased to see that both of you are all right. You mustn't worry. Everything will be fine soon. We'll get all this sorted as soon as we can.'

There was a warmth in his voice that hadn't been there in the courtyard. There he'd been affable, polite. Now he sounded positively friendly. There was also a tone in his voice that Stephen had thought gone forever from the world – he sounded like he knew what he was talking about. And there was something else too, a faint undertone of …

'Do you *know* us?' Kirsten said suddenly, recognising the tone before Stephen did.

The man gave her question some thought.

'That question,' he said, 'raises what you might call metaphysical difficulties. On the one hand I've never seen either of you before in my life. But on the other I do know you, yes. In fact I know you both very well indeed.'

He made a face.

'It's hard to explain now,' he said. 'Please be patient. Nothing bad is going to happen to you, believe me.'

'Why should we?' Stephen said angrily. 'Bad things have happened to us already. Why shouldn't they happen to us again?'

The driver's smile twitched slightly.

'Because I won't let them,' he said softly.

And with a last nod he was gone, closing the door behind him. His smile seemed to linger in the room. Kirsten and Stephen looked at each other. Kirsten had stopped crying.

'He *knows* us!' she said. Then she said it again, because it sounded so strange. She glanced over towards the mirror, and caught a glimpse of her own haggard face.

'Yuck!' she said. 'I look a fright. I'm going to wash my face.'

There was a bathroom at the end of the corridor, but to get to it she'd have to pass the headless man's door. A minute before Stephen couldn't have imagined her doing that; now she positively breezed out of the room. Stephen went to the door and watched her saunter down the hall. The suddenness of the change in her astonished him. But then she'd been like that since they'd met, he supposed – changeable.

The abbot came back up the stairs carrying a steaming bowl of water and, draped over his shoulder, several bath-towels.

'How is the Fräulein?' he asked.

'She seems all right now. She's washing her face.'

'Good,' he said. 'I'm going to leave these things in with our guests. Then I must go and check on the patients. And the monks too, for that matter. I don't know what to expect – or rather I fear I do.'

'I'll go with you,' Stephen said.

'Is that wise? Philip was very upset in the courtyard. He may well direct it at you.'

'He already has.' Stephen told him how Philip had hit him.

The story obviously upset Paul.

'I'd best leave these things in with the strangers,' he said. 'Then I'll … I'll sort things out. Somehow. Philip has got to get a grip on himself. There's too much to do. The patients haven't even been fed this morning.'

He went into the strangers' room, and as he came back out Kirsten emerged from the bathroom. Her face had a pink, scrubbed look. She wasn't exactly smiling, but she was certainly calmer than she'd been earlier.

'Paul,' she said, 'who's looking after the sick people?'

'No one as yet,' the abbot said. 'I was just telling Stephen. We must organise the rest of them. Simon is like a rock, but he can't do everything. I need Thomas. Most of all I need Philip.'

'We have to talk to Philip,' Stephen said, not wanting to. 'He's gone crazy. We have to try to reason with him.'

'Certainly I have to talk to him,' the abbot said. 'As for yourself and the Fräulein … do you think it would be wise?'

He eyed Stephen dubiously. Stephen reluctantly told Kirsten how Philip had hit him. She made a face.

'He was upset,' she said. 'Frightened. He has no *real* reason to fear us – what have we done to him? No, Stephen is right, the sooner we face him and talk some sense into him the better. Maybe I should try. He wouldn't listen to me yesterday, but maybe today– '

'No!' Stephen said. 'Absolutely not! He certainly won't listen to you now!'

Her mood had improved, but that gave her no right to be stupid. Of course, she didn't know about the apparitions yet.

Philip would no doubt have heard Thomas's story by now, he might be every bit as hostile towards Kirsten as he was towards Stephen.

The abbot considered. For the first time since Stephen had met him he seemed unsure.

'I don't like it,' he said. 'But Fräulein Herzenweg is right. We must try to talk to Philip.'

'Then let's do it now,' Kirsten said. 'Before I start getting afraid again.'

Paul hesitated. He looked at Stephen.

'It won't get any easier,' Stephen said.

The abbot nodded.

'Very well,' he said. 'Let's go.'

And they did. But as they went down the stone stairs Stephen brushed his hand across the back pocket of his jeans, where the little silver pistol nestled reassuringly.

25. Agent on the Mend

Becoming conscious again felt peculiar. It was very different from other such returns, like waking from sleep, say, or the slow, tingling passage into flesh in the first place. The body had been technically dead after all, animated only by my friend's efforts.

I felt a tightness around my throat – bandages – and the warmth of two solid lumps in the bandages that I knew were the crystals – healing crystals now.

There was no confusion as such. I knew what must be happening. As to what had happened since I died, that was a different matter. I didn't even know how much time had passed since then. My memory ended with the last thought I'd had as the hunter with the hatchet jumped from the ditch beside me. My body had been groggy from sleep; getting out of the car, I'd seen the hunter's movement only as a blur. Even as I'd turned to unshade him that last thought had gone quite clearly through my mind – the thought that I'd been too slow.

I'd barely had time to deflect the pain, and none at all to deflect the blow itself. I'd known at once that the wound was fatal. I'd concentrated on clinging to the maimed body, hanging on inside until my friend came to help. After that I knew nothing of what took place outside. But I was here now, and the body obviously wasn't dead anymore.

I opened my eyes. There was a peculiar feeling of lightness in the air. I was lying on a bed. My friend sat on a chair beside me. The Sug was sitting at a table, looking petulant and uncomfortable, which is to say he was looking Sug-like.

'Well,' said my friend, 'here you are at last.'

I swallowed carefully. There was no pain. I could feel the crystals' warmth bathing the damaged tissue. My voice, when I tried it, sounded fine – a little hoarse maybe, but under the circumstances that was nothing to complain about.

'What happened?' I asked.

'Well, you remember the ambush don't you?'

'Yes.' A narrow, hedge-lined road on a hill, a morning mist, and a tree felled or fallen across the track in the half-light before dawn. A thought that even mad hunting things surely wouldn't be so very, very stupid.

'There were five of them,' my friend said. 'I got two, and our friend here got the others. They attacked him as ferociously as us, which proves that at least part of his story is true, I suppose. Your head was almost severed. I had to take it off for a while, I'm afraid – it kept flopping all over the place as we drove.'

'That's all right,' I said. Then I laughed as a thought struck me. 'I wasn't very attached to it anyway,' I said.

My friend smiled.

'No,' he said. 'Not at the time.'

Then he laughed too.

'You should have seen the look on your face, though,' he said.

'Hold on,' I said. 'Why am I laughing? I feel ... *giddy*. Is it the damage to the body?'

'It's the atmosphere here, I think. I feel the same.'

'But where are we?'

My friend was smiling again.

'We're in the place our friend here talked about – the abbey. And he was right: there are people here, humans.'

'Is that possible?'

My friend shrugged.

'Maybe not,' he said. 'But they're here.'

It made no sense at all. We'd cleared the area thoroughly and established a barrier no force known to humans could penetrate. Even now their scientists and soldiers sat baffled and furious outside it.

'So the rest of his story may be true too,' I said.

The Sug spoke for the first time.

'I told you,' he said with some bitterness. 'I *swore* I was telling the truth.'

'Tut tut!' my friend said. 'You can hardly blame us for doubting you.'

The Sug sighed.

'No,' he said. 'I can't.'

In itself that was a remarkable admission for a Sug. This one had been in a peculiar mood since we met. Moods, I should say, because he swung from one extreme to the other. I mean it was extreme even by Sug standards, which is really saying something. No amount of Sug pride could hide from him the calamity his people's foolishness had almost caused, but at times he seemed almost annoyed by his own humility. Anger and resentment and humility and fear would flash out of him unpredictably, and something else that in anyone but a Sug I'd have called guilt. A Sug with a conscience – now that would be one for the books.

'So,' I said to my friend, 'a complication. Tell me, how are the humans taking all this?'

'Guess.'

'I imagine they're petrified.'

'I'd call that an understatement.'

'What did they think when they saw me?' I asked. 'It must have … surprised them.'

A smile crossed my friend's face at the memory.

'You could certainly say that,' he said. 'One of them just ran away. The others wanted to. Really, it was almost like the good old days. You wouldn't remember.'

I looked at the Sug, a big glowering lump at the table.

'What about you?' I asked him. 'It can't be much fun for you, stuck right in the middle of your favourite species.'

The Sug made a disgusted face.

'I thought I'd remembered how foul they were,' he said. 'I was wrong. My stomach heaves just sitting here.'

I felt no sympathy for him. His people had caused this mess. He'd been a part of it.

'The people here killed those hunters we saw yesterday,' my friend said. 'The ones in the town. All in all, we got eight more. According to what our friend the Sug tells us, that leaves only four. They'll be on their way here now.'

He gestured about him.

'Do you know where we are?' he asked.

'This … abbey. In the mountains you said.'

'Yes, but do you know where this abbey *is*?'

'No.'

My friend gave a dry little chuckle.

'You do, you know,' he said. 'Think about it.'

I did. I thought about my giddiness, about the odd lightness in the atmosphere. I drew in my breath suddenly.

'It can't be the crystal works!' I said.

'It is, you know,' my friend said. 'This abbey is built on the royal mound. The birthing lake is right outside the walls.'

'But the crystals are dead in the world!'

'They were, but they don't seem to be dead now. They're not fully active, but they're not dead either. Something is going on here, and it's not of our doing.'

I looked suspiciously at the Sug.

'Don't look at *him*!' my friend said. 'The Sug always hated this place. It hurts him to be here at all!'

'But how can this be?'

'Don't ask me. The world does what it wants to, as they say. But whatever is going on here, I think it's what kept these humans free from our clearance.'

My mind raced with the implications of the news. I calmed it down. First things first: we had a job to do. If the crystal works were in any way active it would only increase our power.

But the power we'd been sent with was plenty in any case. There were only the killings to be finished. The presence of humans, grotesque and bizarre though it was, was just a complication. We could deal with it if they just kept out of the way. I hated loose ends. My friend always calls me finicky.

'The humans ran away,' I said. 'Do you think that means they'll stay out of our way while we're working?'

My friend gave a little shrug, holding both hands up in a gesture of ignorance.

'Your guess is as good as mine,' he said. 'I didn't say all of them ran, I said they wanted to. There's one that struck me as a possible problem. He felt dangerous. Their leader, though, is quite civilised, at least by human standards. Of course that mightn't work to our advantage when the killing starts. I don't know, we may have to subdue them all. Certainly I expect some trouble.'

As if on cue there was the sound of a gun being fired somewhere outside. My friend turned towards the window.

'Oh dear,' he said wearily. 'I think it's arrived.'

26. The Old Monk

Kirsten, Paul and Stephen crossed the courtyard and went towards the abbey's main doors. But before they reached them the old monk, Brother Simon, came out. He was still holding his shotgun.

'Paul!' he called. 'I was coming to look for you.'

He started speaking rapidly in French to the abbot. Beyond the odd word here and there, Stephen couldn't understand a thing. But Kirsten listened with obvious understanding to the old man's words and the abbot's replies. After a while she joined in the conversation. Philip's name was mentioned repeatedly. Whenever it came from the lips of the old monk, the name was said with undisguised distaste.

Finally the abbot turned to Stephen.

'Trouble,' he said simply.

'Philip?'

The abbot indicated the old monk.

'Simon is as good a judge of men as I've ever known,' he said. 'He thinks Philip is extremely dangerous right now. Thomas is too terrified to help, but he won't make trouble.

They're both in the refectory, our diningroom. Philip is waving his gun around and mouthing nonsense about the devil and his works being invited into the monastery.'

The old monk, Simon, spoke directly to Stephen for the first time.

'You figure prominently in Philip's list of the devil's works,' he said. 'I'd avoid him if I were you, for everyone's sake.'

'And me?' Kirsten asked. 'Has he said anything about me?'

The old monk cocked an eyebrow at her.

'Oddly enough, Fräulein,' he said, 'he didn't mention you, at least not while I was there. But I didn't stay very long. The sight of peasant superstition spilling out of an unbalanced mind is a spectacle I find particularly unedifying.'

The dry irony of his voice was actually reassuring. There was a solidity about Brother Simon. Here, you felt, was a man who would react to what was in front of his eyes, no more and no less. And he'd certainly seemed stolid earlier, in the court-yard, refusing to give in to emotional weakness when the thing that was in front of his eyes had terrified everyone else who saw it.

'One thing is certain,' Paul said, looking at Stephen. 'You must avoid Philip. If he's so fixated on you we'll never calm him down while you're there.'

Stephen knew he was right, but he didn't want to let Kirsten face the maddened monk either. Paul would try to defend her if it came to violence, but when all was said and done he was a monk, and Stephen didn't believe he'd use physical means. He realised suddenly that he himself had decided to shoot Philip if he had to, if Philip tried to use his own gun on any of them. It seemed the situation might reach a point where there was no other option. Yesterday in the library he'd hesitated to use the pistol; today he'd no intention of making the same mistake, especially if Kirsten was threatened. He felt a sudden fierce protectiveness towards her.

The abbot seemed to guess what he was thinking.

'I won't let Philip hurt Fräulein Herzenweg,' he said. 'You have my word on that.'

Stephen stood undecided.

'There is much to be done,' Simon said. 'Whatever is happening, the sick people must be tended to. Why don't you help me do that?'

Stephen was torn. But facing Philip might bring on the very crisis they all feared.

'All right,' he said to Simon.

'Good,' Simon said. 'You can help me get the food ready. Come.'

Stephen took a last look at Kirsten.

'Be very careful,' he said.

'I got on well with Philip until yesterday,' she said. 'I don't believe he'll hurt me. Anyway, Paul will protect me, won't you, Paul?'

The abbot's smile didn't look very genuine, but his voice was sincere.

'I will,' he said.

Stephen followed Simon towards the kitchen wing. On the way Simon scanned the courtyard.

'There should be a pistol here somewhere,' he said.

'I got it already. It's in my pocket.'

Simon smiled for the first time since Stephen had met him. It was a grim little smile that suited what Stephen had seen of his personality.

'You're a sensible boy,' Simon said.

When they reached the kitchens, Simon pointed out a great iron pot of cold broth on the big cooking range. 'If you start heating the broth,' he said, 'I'll go and check on the patients.'

'Do you normally look after them?'

'Normally,' Simon said, 'I look after the bell-ringing. It's a foolish practise in my opinion, but it's a standard thing with us. But now of course things are not normal. Since all this began I've been doing most of the feeding. Luckily even the most disturbed of our patients eats with no trouble. Thomas helps sometimes, but he's young, and the patients are … well, at best they're very *strange*. Mostly I have Thomas fix the food, and I dispense it.'

After Simon left to go upstairs, Stephen found matches in a drawer and lit the burner under the pot. Then he looked in cupboards till he found one full of bowls. He put four of them on a big tray and went looking for spoons. He was worried about Kirsten. He'd been foolish to let her face Philip without him. The thought of the broth reminded him that he hadn't eaten since yesterday morning. He felt suddenly weak, almost nauseous. The weight of the morning's events seemed to hit him all at once. He sat weakly on to a chair by the table. His head throbbed.

Then the shot sounded. It was muffled by the stone walls, but some part of Stephen's mind had been listening for it all along.

He jumped up and ran. Behind him he heard the clatter of the chair hitting the stone floor. Somewhere ahead he heard Simon's hurried steps descending the stairs. Stephen didn't wait for the old monk. He ran on, pulling the little pistol from his back pocket as he went.

27. The Body in the Refectory

The second shot rang out as Stephen crossed the courtyard. At the sound of it he ran faster. Behind him he heard Simon call out, but he didn't look back. Then another voice hailed him. He couldn't make out the words it said, but its effect on him was as immediate as it was bizarre – he stopped in mid-run, frozen, with one foot raised. He couldn't make his body move at all.

Only his head could move freely. He turned to look for the owner of the second voice. He saw the man who'd been driving the car, the friendly stranger. He was walking unhurriedly towards Stephen, his hands in his coat pockets.

'You can't interfere,' he called out. 'It's not allowed.'

Simon came up behind Stephen at a trot, carrying his shot-gun. He passed him with a puzzled glance, but didn't stop. As Simon disappeared through the doors of the bell-tower the driver reached Stephen and gently touched his arm. Stephen could move again. He glared at the driver, who stood looking calmly at him.

'I'm sorry,' the driver said. 'But you mustn't interfere in anything that happens between the monks.'

'And what if it's Kirsten who's been shot?' Stephen spat angrily.

'Then it doesn't really matter.'

The cold-bloodedness of the remark almost made Stephen gasp. But he was distracted by the sight of Kirsten herself coming into the courtyard. She was almost staggering, but there was no sign of a wound. She was crying as she came up to them, her face ugly with distress.

'Paul's been shot,' she sobbed. 'I think he's dead.'

The driver clicked his tongue. 'Oh my!' he said. 'More complications!'

Stephen turned on him like a dog.

'*Complications?*' he hissed. 'That lunatic has shot the abbot, and you call it a *complication?*'

Kirsten caught his arm.

'You don't understand,' she said. 'It was you who started it.'

'*Me?*'

'Well, it was an *image* of you. I know you weren't there, but ... but you were. You just *appeared*, standing beside me, and Philip panicked. He tried to shoot you.'

Stephen was appalled.

'No!' he said. But it must be true. He remembered his weakness in the kitchen. So it had been more than simple shock or hunger.

'The bullet seemed to hit the thing,' Kirsten said. 'But it had no effect. Paul hadn't seen the image. He thought Philip was firing at me. He grabbed Philip and tried to wrestle the pistol away from him. The gun went off, and Paul was shot in the chest.'

'And the image?'

'It just disappeared. It stood there for a moment, looking at Paul as he fell. Then it just ... it just *went out*, like a light.'

Simon came back out. His face was tight.

'The abbot is alive,' he said, 'for now. But Philip is gone again.'

Stephen couldn't accept that Paul lay dying a few metres away. He'd expected Philip to turn violent, but not against the abbot. It could only have been an accident.

'Where did Philip go?' he asked Simon.

'When I got there he was kneeling over the abbot, sobbing. Telling him he was sorry, if you please. It's a bit late for that, I told him. I took a look at Paul, and Philip ran off.'

'And Thomas?'

Simon made a face.

'I saw no sign of that foolish boy at all.'

'And Paul's alive?' Kirsten said. She sounded like she didn't believe it.

'Not for long,' Simon said. 'It's a serious chest wound, and he's losing a lot of blood.'

'Can't you do anything for him?'

Simon shook his head.

'We have first-aid equipment here, but nothing that would cope with wounds like this – you don't get many gunshot wounds in a monastery, you know.'

The driver had listened to all of this in silence. Now Kirsten stood in front of him and looked harshly into his bland guarded eyes. Her face was still wet with tears, but the news that the abbot wasn't actually dead seemed to have galvanised her. The driver looked back at her mildly.

'You must do something,' she said to him.

He shook his head.

'That's not possible,' he said. 'I cannot interfere.'

'You've already interfered,' she said. 'That's what started all this, isn't it?'

He looked sharply at her. So did Stephen. Did she know something, or was she guessing?

'If you can help the abbot,' Simon said, 'then you must do it.'

He too spoke mildly, but he hefted his gun meaningfully. The stranger ignored him, keeping his eyes on Kirsten's. His eyes had lost their mask of blandness now.

Kirsten stared back at him with a look every bit as hard as his own.

'Do it,' she said – ordered, rather.

'This is very bad,' the driver said. 'You don't realise what you're asking me to do.'

Without breaking eye contact, Kirsten pointed at Stephen.

'The appearance of *his* image was directly responsible for Paul being shot,' she said.

The driver turned and considered Stephen thoughtfully. It struck Stephen that the man was taking the whole matter of the double very calmly.

'Oh dear, oh dear,' the driver said. 'This really is very bad. And just when everything seemed to be going so well too.'

'The abbot is dying,' Kirsten said insistently. 'If you can sew a man's head back on then you can help a man with a gunshot wound.'

'It's not the same thing at all, at all!' the driver snapped. 'Maybe I could help him, and maybe I couldn't. It's never been tried. We only need these bodies for short-term purposes. Presumably the abbot would require his for rather longer.'

Stephen felt his skin crawl at the words, but the others showed no reaction. Kirsten held the driver's stare.

'You have to try,' she persisted.

The driver exhaled slowly through his teeth. For the first time since his arrival he seemed unsure of himself.

'I'll have to talk to my colleague,' he said.

'Do then,' said Kirsten. 'And hurry.'

The man gave a shrug. Then he turned and without another word went back across the courtyard.

'You're joking,' I said to my friend.

'The girl is right,' he said doggedly. 'This would never have happened but for our interference.'

I glared across to where the Sug sat glowering at us.

'*Their* interference, you mean,' I said.

'That makes no difference to her. And she has a point. Besides, he helped us. We have certain obligations.'

It would have been too much to expect that the Sug would stay out of it.

'You're insane,' he growled. 'It is not permitted to interfere with human affairs. Let them all shoot each other if it come to it, the more the merrier.'

My friend raised a contemptuous eyebrow.

'You can always rely on a Sug for a reasonable contribution to a debate,' he sneered. 'My friend here is right – it was *your* people who got us into this mess. If the human dies it will be as a direct result of *your* interference in our legitimate business. Who are you to talk about rights and wrongs?'

The Sug flushed. While my friend was gone I'd tried to coax some conversation out of him, but he'd only grunted responses to my remarks. Still, I was starting to feel some little bit of sympathy for him. His truculence wasn't merely because his mission had failed. It wasn't even simply the presence of humans. These things would have been bad enough, but the nature of this place itself was making him uncomfortable. Even the sleepy, formless sort of power it was giving out now would be unpleasant to him. What I felt as a lightness in the air he'd experience as something very close to pain.

Now he cracked. His reserve broke, and he spluttered almost incoherently.

'How were we supposed to know what it was like here now?' he demanded. 'It's completely poisoned with their human foulness! My creatures were mad from the moment we arrived. They tried to kill me as soon as I materialised. I was so sick I thought I was dying – not just the body, but *me*! Nobody warned me to expect anything like that!'

I felt some real pity for him. A very small bit of pity, admittedly, but pity nonetheless. After all, he too was only an agent, and he must have genuinely suffered. It was a measure of the Sugs' toughness that he'd managed to stick it out at all.

But my friend just snorted.

'Listen to yourself!' he jeered. He imitated the Sug in a high, whining voice, 'Nobody told me! How was I supposed to know!'

Then he resumed his own flat tone.

'Your people could have known in the same way that we know,' he said, his voice frigid with anger. 'By learning. But oh no, the Sug are too proud, too squeamish. They'd prefer to sit sulking in a corner of Nowhere for ten thousand years and think up ways to interfere with us! If you'd asked, maybe we'd have shared our information with you – but again, no, the Sug ask no favours of anyone. So, as usual, you learn the hard way, too late, and you make it hard for everyone else too. And when it goes wrong you find someone else to pin the blame on – also as usual. Send an agent here for the first time in two thousand years, and then have the gall to be surprised that it's changed! Well, excuse me, but I never heard anything so preposterous!'

The Sug hung his head and said nothing. I stood up.

'Enough squabbling!' I said. 'We have to decide what to do, and soon. The human is dying.'

I looked to the Sug again.

'When we've done here,' I said, 'we can erase every sign of our presence. We can erase memory of us from the humans' minds. Those outside the barrier haven't a clue what's happening in here. We can leave them with a mystery, regrettable though that is. What we *can't* leave is a dead human, not if we can possibly help it. That's not for their sake, it's for our own.'

The Sug winced at the mention of the barrier. It was too tangible a proof of the power we now had in the world.

'You can wipe out their memories?' he asked. 'You can really do that, selectively?'

I understood his doubt. Erasing memories is no great trick. The tricky bit is to do it without turning your subject into a vegetable. Such delicate work wasn't really a Sug type of thing, though among my people the Sug were famous for their selective memories.

'Yes,' I told him. 'We can.'

'And you really think you can help the human?'

'I've no idea. There's no technical reason why not. It's only a body after all.'

'I must admit I'd like to help the human anyway,' my friend said. 'I've had a look inside him. He's a good man.'

The Sug made an automatic sound of disgust at the very idea. To him the concept of a 'good man' was a contradiction in terms. I was a bit shocked myself to hear the note of grudging respect in my friend's voice. He doesn't hate humans, anymore than I do. In many ways they've progressed a lot since the old days, and anyway hatred is a wasteful thing. But there's a distinct difference between not hating humans and feeling something positive towards them. They're a dangerous species, without manners or even much self-respect, even harder to like than the Sug.

'This arguing is just wasting time,' I said. 'Do I take it we're going to help if we can?'

'Yes,' my friend said.

I looked to the Sug again.

'You can lodge a formal objection,' I said.

The Sug looked shocked. Any objection he raised would of course have no weight. But I was treating him with the kind of formal courtesy the Sug delight in. And I was offering him a way to save face – nobody could blame him for anything that might come of our actions if he lodged a formal protest beforehand.

The Sug mightn't have expected the courtesy, but in the end

it was me who was surprised. He didn't take the easy way out.

'No,' he said bitterly. 'I find the action you intend most distasteful, but you're right. The Sug made a big mistake here. We were foolish to do it. Only you can do anything now to rectify the error. If you think assisting the human will improve the situation then you must try to help him. In fact, as a representative of the Sug race I'd like to formally request your assistance in the matter.'

It was a remarkable statement coming from a Sug. A historic statement, in fact. His people and mine had agreed on very little in the last ten thousand years. If you got right down to it, we weren't exactly chummy before that either. In all of our histories there was only one big thing – apart from the obvious – that we'd successfully collaborated on, one thing we'd managed to persuade them to do. And though they'd kept the agreement made then after their fashion, they'd never really forgiven us for it. Which was, of course, just like them.

I loosened the bandages on my neck until I could slide the crystal pebbles out. The quartz veins were burning brightly now in the dull stone, nearly purring with their full power. The Sug eyed them nervously. They had nothing like this, and they coveted this power even as they feared it.

'They're very bright now,' the Sug said.

'Of course,' said my friend, his voice gentle. 'They've come home.'

Home. The word had a unique aching beauty. When any of us, even a Sug, says the word in any language, you can hear the loss and yearning in their voice. We who had no place in the world to call our home had strayed here where once we had walked. And these crystals, which had been born in this very place, were going to be used – with the consent and encouragement of a Sug – to help a human.

My friend read my mind.

'It's a funny old world,' he said.

'It is,' said the Sug.

I looked at them. We were all aware of the importance of the moment. You appreciate that type of thing when you live outside time. I licked my lips.

'Well, folks,' I said. 'Let's go make some history.'

We went.

29. The Hunters Outside

The refectory was a large room with a long wooden table at its centre. In front of the table the abbot lay on his back, his arms outstretched. His thin face was chalk white. The front of his dark habit was darker with a wet spreading stain.

Simon was kneeling silently by the dying abbot, his eyes fixed on the still white face. Stephen stood by, feeling useless. He kept glancing towards the doorway, expecting Philip to burst in at any moment. It wasn't just that he feared the big monk – he did – but he was more angry than anything else. There was a lot of strain on all of them. Thomas hadn't managed to cope, but it was only Philip who'd cracked and resorted to physical violence.

After a while, when there was no sign of either Philip or the strangers, claustrophobia got the better of Stephen. He wanted to be doing *something*. He was almost tempted to go looking for Philip, to force the confrontation that it seemed must come. In a way he felt guilty. It was his image after all that had provoked the shooting – his image, though not, consciously at least, his doing. He should take his pistol and face Philip down, for better or for worse. Thinking of the big man's expertise, and of his willingness to shoot, Stephen guessed that it would be for worse. But it seemed somehow his responsibility. He said as much to Simon.

'Don't be foolish,' Simon said, without taking his eyes off the abbot. 'That's pride talking.'

'*Pride*?' Simon couldn't have picked a word that surprised him more.

'Yes. Pride. None of us is responsible for any of this. Even Philip – though it galls me to admit it – isn't responsible. He's mad with fear. We're *not* mad with fear, but that doesn't mean we're not afraid. None of this is our doing. Blaming yourself for it is just another way of making yourself out to be more important than you are.'

Stephen had to admit that he hadn't thought of it like that, but maybe Simon had a point. It didn't exactly make him feel better, but it let him forget about confronting Philip. He'd felt he ought to do it, but that didn't mean he'd been looking forward to it – he was in no hurry to die.

Instead he went looking for Kirsten, who hadn't been able to face the sight of the dying abbot. He walked along with his eyes and ears alert for any sounds. Steeling your nerve to face up to Philip was one thing, running into him rounding a corner was another thing entirely.

He found Kirsten in the courtyard. She was standing by the gates, looking out, and she didn't look happy. Stephen went over.

'What is it?' he asked.

'There's someone out there,' she said without looking at him. 'Another sick person, maybe.'

'No. There's more than one. I've seen two now, and they move far too carefully for my liking.'

He followed her gaze. Even as he looked he saw a figure scurry across the path that led down the hill from the gates. It happened too fast to make out any detail. The figure emerged from the long grass on one side of the path and disappeared into a stand of trees on the other side.

He saw what Kirsten meant. The figure hadn't wandered across, but moved furtively and deliberately like an animal crossing exposed space.

'This is trouble,' he said.

'Not at all,' said a cheery voice behind them. 'This is good news.'

The strangers from the car had come up silently and stood watching them. The man who'd spoken was the man Stephen had last seen as a headless monstrosity. He wasn't headless now. His coat and shirt were gone, and he stood there, bare-chested, with a bandaged neck. A shivery feeling ran through Stephen when he looked at the bandages, but apart from that there was nothing disturbing about the man. He was younger and slighter than the other two, and his smiling face looked friendly. His eyes were grey and clear, and they looked at Stephen and Kirsten with open curiosity. The driver stood calmly beside him with his hands in his pockets, while the third stranger hung back behind. He was the only one who didn't look friendly, but even he no longer looked quite so sour.

'Should we close the gates?' Stephen asked.

The re-headed man shook his head.

'They won't come in,' he said. 'We'll have to go and get them later.'

'*Get* them?' Kirsten said. 'Do you know what those things *are*?'

'Well, yes,' he said, 'I do. We've gathered them here precisely because we know what they are.'

'And what do you intend doing with them?' Kirsten demanded. She seemed to have no fear any more of the strangers. Stephen envied her. He felt that no amount of reassurance could make him feel at ease with them. They were just too strange.

'I asked you a question,' Kirsten snapped. 'If those things out there are like the ones who attacked us yesterday, then they're very dangerous. You say you've gathered them here – to do what exactly?'

The man smiled at her with what looked like real affection.

'Why,' he said, 'to exterminate them, of course.'

Kirsten hadn't been expecting that.

'Oh!' she said.

The driver had heard enough banter.

'Come now,' he said. 'We can't waste time in idle chatter. There's work to be done. This isn't over yet.'

But looking at these most peculiar but very confident men, Stephen thought that maybe, somehow, it was. For all their strangeness they were the only people he'd seen lately who seemed to know exactly what they were doing. He still didn't trust them – but it might be a case of having to.

30. The Bread and the Cheese

In the refectory the abbot was lying as Stephen had last seen him, although there was no sign of Simon. The driver and the bandaged man knelt on either side of Paul, each putting one hand on his chest. The third man stood beside them, looking on. On his face was a very odd look, a mixture of fascination and disgust. Stephen and Kirsten stood by.

There were footsteps in the corridor. Stephen turned, ready, he hoped, for anything. But it was only Simon who came in. He was scowling, though his face lightened when he saw the two strangers kneeling beside the abbot. The two men were as still as the dying man himself. They might have been carved out of stone. There was an identical expression on their faces, a distant trance-like look.

'I found Philip,' Simon said in a low voice.

'Where?' Kirsten asked.

'We keep a chapel here for those who are inclined to use it. He's there now, praying and crying for forgiveness. I still haven't found Thomas though. He's probably hiding under a bed somewhere.'

'Philip still has his gun?' Stephen asked.

Simon sneered.

'His gun is in his hand. A most obscene combination if you ask me – beating your breast and asking for forgiveness with a pistol in your hand. He's grabbed a big crucifix and he's praying at that. I never liked having a crucifix there at all, it seemed like an insult to our non-Christian Brothers, myself included. But Paul felt it helped some of them concentrate. Well, Philip is certainly concentrating on it now.'

He grimaced in disgust.

'I never trusted that man,' he said. 'He had too much hate bottled up inside him. Hatred for himself. It was bound to explode one day. If it hadn't been this that caused it, then it would have been something else. I said it more than once to Paul, but accepting people at face value is Paul's way.'

'It's not himself that Philip hates now,' Stephen said glumly. 'It's us – it's me.'

'Bah!' Simon said. 'That's how self-hate works, you push it out onto someone else.'

The strangers hadn't moved a muscle in minutes. Simon looked at the silent tableau on the floor as though to distract himself from his own anger. He nodded towards the bare-chested stranger.

'I must say,' he said, 'that man seems to have made a remarkable recovery. Maybe there's hope for the abbot yet. But it's not good. I've seen a lot of gunshot wounds in my time.'

He turned to Stephen with a sudden sharp look.

'Do you still have that pistol?' he asked.

'I do.'

'Do you think you'll be able to use it?'

'I don't know.'

Simon pursed his lips.

'I killed my first man in 1944,' Simon said. 'August twelfth. Twenty past ten on a beautiful summer evening. I was older than you, but not a whole lot. The man was a German soldier – only a boy himself, come to that.'

'Was it hard to do?'

'It was very hard to *make* myself do it. I kept telling myself that he deserved it, that he was an invader. They were cruel invaders, the Germans. They'd killed many of my friends – tortured them and killed them. But that fellow was just a fellow like myself when all was said and done. At another time we might have been friends. I always rather liked the Germans, really.'

'How did you manage to make yourself kill him then?'

'He saw me. He saw my gun. I knew that he'd kill me – he'd been trained not to have qualms, and he'd fought before. So it was him or me. And when it came down to it, I didn't want it to be me.'

He nodded, remembering.

'He was eating bread and cheese when we crept up on him,' he said. 'After he was dead, I saw the bread lying on the ground. The marks of his teeth were still in it. It's funny what you notice at times like that. They were hungry times. I picked up the bread, tore off the bloody bits and threw them away. But when I went to eat it I saw the marks of his teeth and I thought that I'd killed him and that those teeth would never bite bread again, and I couldn't eat it.'

'But you killed again afterwards?'

Simon shrugged.

'Sometimes what *you* feel like doing isn't so important,' he said. 'Sometimes you simply have a job to do. You have the right to have fear, the right – the duty, I'd say – to feel qualms, but not the right to endanger others whose lives and well-being depend on your actions. So you do whatever it takes.'

'And you did it?'

Again Simon shrugged. His face had the look of a man who'd seen much that he didn't want to see.

'I couldn't eat the bread,' he said. 'But I did eat the cheese. Like I say, they were hungry times.'

Stephen turned to Kirsten, to see what she might have made of Simon's story.

But Kirsten wasn't there.

Stephen looked around desperately. She wasn't in the room. He turned to the third stranger.

'The girl!' he said frantically. 'Where did she go?'

The man gestured at the open door, puzzled by Stephen's intensity.

Simon realised what was wrong. He said something in a foreign language that sounded like a most un-monkish curse.

'The little fool!' he hissed. 'She's gone to the chapel to try and talk sense to that madman! He'll kill her for sure!'

The big stranger obviously understood now. He was out the door, running, before either Stephen or Simon had time to take a step.

31. The Corpse in the Chapel

The big stranger moved with incredible speed for a man of his size. By the time Stephen got outside the door, the corridor was already empty. He turned to Simon, who was at his heels.

'Where's the chapel?' Stephen said.

Simon took the lead, jogging off down the passage. Stephen followed, his heart pounding in his chest. At every step he expected to hear a shot. They rounded corners and went down passageways. The running footsteps of the big stranger were always just ahead of them. Then suddenly they were silent, and rounding another corner Stephen saw big double doors standing open ahead. They were odd doors, one made of a dark wood, almost black, the other light and bright. Stephen and Simon went through the doors with their guns at the ready.

The place was a largely bare room that looked nothing like Stephen's idea of a chapel, but he didn't take in any details right then. He only saw the three figures standing in the middle of the room. Furthest from them was Philip, standing in front of a large squared block of dark stone that had to be the altar. He looked as though he'd risen from his knees on he[ar]ing someone enter. His gun was held tightly in on[e] the other he held a big wooden crucifix, and it was this rather than the gun that he held out threateningly towards them. Kirsten stood a few steps away from him, holding out her empty hands as she said his name softly.

'Philip,' she said. 'Please!'

The big stranger had stopped about halfway between Kirsten and the doorway. Philip's eyes were on him as Simon and Stephen came in. They were eyes quite mad with terror. He shouted at them in a strangled voice that was hardly human in spite of the fact that it formed words.

'*Devils!*' he shrieked. 'Devils! Do you come for me now?'

His eyes shifted to the newcomers. Stephen watched the gun in his hand, wishing that Kirsten and the stranger would get out of the way. He thought of what Simon had said – you have the right to be afraid. Right or no right, he was terrified now, though whether he was more terrified of shooting or of being shot it was hard to say. Still, he felt that, one way or another, the resolution of this thing had come.

'For God's sake, Philip,' Kirsten said in an entreating voice. The voice tried to sound calm, but it trembled.

Philip's eyes rolled madly back at her.

'*God?*' he hissed. 'You say His name, witch? The tongue will wit our blaspheming mouth!'

hed the crucifix at her as though it were some

. Indeed in Philip's hands it *was* a weapon,

ded purpose. Kirsten flinched, maybe

t to hit her with it. Philip grimaced in a

'See now,' he said. 'It frightens you, does it? Truth at last!'

'The idiot thinks he's in a horror film,' Simon hissed in a low voice. Aloud, he called, 'Philip! Put down your weapon! I order you as your acting superior!'

Again the crazy eyes flicked back towards Stephen and Simon.

'My superior?' Philip said. 'My superior?'

He slowly raised the big black pistol. Stephen's fingers tightened on the grip of his own gun. But Philip only raised the gun to display it. He held it up beside his face, its muzzle pointing at the ceiling, its sleek ugly blackness rubbing against his cheek.

'My superior is dead!' he said. 'My superior and my friend. This is what killed him. It was in my hand when it killed him, but it wasn't me who did it. Oh no! It wasn't me.'

Simon made a disgusted noise.

'Philip,' Kirsten said, 'Paul isn't dead. Nobody killed him. He's going to be all right.'

'Liar!' Philip roared. 'They're dead! They're all dead! But it wasn't me. It wasn't me who did it!'

He was looking at the pistol now, the cold black metal inches from his demented eyes. The eyes moved slowly over the gun-barrel. It was as if he'd never seen such a thing before and was trying to guess what it was. For those few moments he seemed to forget them all. It was a macabre sight, the way he crouched there by the altar, animal-like, with his crucifix and his gun.

They all stood as still as Philip, almost afraid to breathe.

The tension that flowed from him seemed to fill the chapel. The man was like a primed bomb – any move might set him off. It was going to happen anyway, Stephen was certain of that. Simon's shotgun would be useless, he couldn't dare shoot for fear of hitting Kirsten or the big stranger. There was only one other weapon in the room apart from Philip's, and that was the one Stephen now held in his hand. Whether they all lived or died was almost certainly going to depend on him, on his ability to make himself shoot the demented monk.

The big stranger turned his head slightly to look at Stephen from the corner of his eye.

'I will do this thing for you, Tellene,' he said.

Stephen blinked. *Tellene?* He remembered the attacker in the library who had snarled some word at him that he hadn't understood. A word that had sounded something like 'ten'. Was that it: tellene? And what did it mean?

The big stranger's eyes flicked back to Philip. The monk was still looking at his pistol. His eyes, Stephen thought, were more frightening than anything he'd seen since he'd woken here; and if he'd seen anything scarier in that other life, the one he couldn't remember, then he didn't want to know about it. He wondered what Philip saw through those eyes when he looked at them – demons and devils, it seemed.

Those mad eyes turned slowly now to focus on Stephen. Stephen read in them, as plainly as though it had been printed there, the message he already knew: the time had come.

'You,' Philip said. His voice was very, very quiet. Stephen's mouth was dry.

'You!' Philip said again, a little louder.

Stephen felt sweat in his palm where it held the plastic grip of the little pistol. *Bread and cheese*, he found himself thinking. *Bread and cheese*. Squeamishness baulks at the bread; prudence eats the cheese. Stay alive.

'You!' Philip said again, in a voice like the hissing of snakes. 'It was *you* who made me kill my friend. You and your devil works!'

It happened then. It was as though someone had tripped a switch.

The hand holding the crucifix dropped it. The hand holding the gun moved out and down. As the gun-barrel dipped, Simon cursed and raised his shotgun pointlessly. Stephen ducked to his left, looking for a clear shot, hoping that he could make himself pull the trigger.

In the end, neither Stephen nor Simon contributed anything to the result. It was the big stranger who, true to his word, took care of it.

Even with the speed he'd already shown, he was too far from Philip and Kirsten to touch either of them in time. But he didn't even try. Instead he raised his right arm and swept it off to one side. Kirsten was thrown through the air, out of harm's way. She squealed in surprise, collapsing to her knees on the ground where she landed. At the same time the stranger thrust the splayed fingers of his left hand straight at Philip. Philip reacted as though he'd been hit by something big and heavy – like a stone wall. He was slammed back against the altar, yelping in fright. The gun fired. Stephen flinched. The sound of the shot boomed and echoed around the stone chapel.

Simon stood staring with his mouth open. Philip didn't move at all. His head rested against the altar, the backs of his heels on the floor. Between these two extremities his body was rigid as a plank. He seemed frozen in the posture he'd been standing in, his hand extended and the pistol now pointing up at the roof. His eyes were staring crazily at some point on the ceiling. His mouth was caught in an ugly snarl.

'Don't hurt him,' the stranger said. 'He's alive, but he's harmless now.'

Something in his voice made Stephen look at him, and he saw where Philip's bullet had lodged. The stranger's hand was clasped to his chest. A dark stain was spreading around it. Kirsten gasped when she saw it. He lowered his hand, and the stain spread rapidly – unnaturally so. The other three stared.

'Please,' the stranger said, 'don't concern yourselves. I've speeded up the heart a little. It will end all this sooner.'

He sounded almost relieved.

'But you'll die!' Simon said.

The stranger smiled for the first time since they'd met him.

'Yes,' he said simply.

The blood covered his chest now. He was getting paler even as they watched. He gestured towards Philip.

'The other two will take care of him,' he said. 'He'll stay frozen until they release him.'

His blood started to drip. He looked down.

'Sorry about messing up the floor,' he said. 'It will be all right later.'

No one replied to his crazy apology. They watched him in silence.

'I want this,' he said. 'I don't want to be here anymore.'

There was a chair beside him. He sat on it heavily, weakening now. He looked at Stephen.

'I owe you and this … this young lady an apology,' he said. Turning to Kirsten, he smiled again.

'Tell the other two that my report will tell the truth. Tell them that this is a token of my good will. And tell them that I'm sorry I deceived them – I did have a little power left.'

He slumped suddenly in the seat. There was no need to check for a pulse. He was obviously dead. And his smile, if anything, was wider.

32. Agents of Mercy

The prospect of helping the human wasn't disgusting in itself, just ... very odd. But it did involve one thing that most of our people would have found obnoxious – we had to communicate with what humans would call his 'soul', an intimacy most of our kind would have found unthinkable with a human. I can't say that it sounded like an attractive idea at the time, the most I can say is that it didn't sound as awful as it once would have.

In the back of my mind I did feel a certain distaste, maybe even fear. The whole thing smelled of danger and of the risk of contamination. If my friend felt any doubts he didn't show them. As we began to search inside the human, it was my friend's calmness that helped me to keep my mind focused on what we had to do.

I felt the spirit almost immediately. The feeling was nowhere near as bad as I'd expected. When all was said and done it was simply a wounded soul in need of help. I soon forgot everything except the job in hand.

The spirit was grieving, but not because of the damage done to its body. It grieved for the whole situation, and for the anguish being felt by the human who'd damaged it. At first, when it noticed our presence, it mistook us for some entities from the mythology of its species, something it called 'angels'. These seemed to be benign imaginary creatures from some fantastic spirit world. The spirit seemed relieved when we assured it that we were not from the supernatural realm.

The abbot's spirit recognised that our intentions were peaceful. We directed its energy towards healing itself. It was ignorant of the processes involved, but it responded to our guidance as best it could.

The body's wound was bad, some of the vital organs had been critically damaged. But there was nothing that seemed impossible to repair. We taught the spirit how to slow the bloodflow and soothe the ruptured tissue. Its untrained efforts would be weak, but they'd concentrate the spirit's attention on its home, which was the important thing. The crystals could repair the flesh, but if the spirit, in its ignorance, lost its grip on the body, there was little or nothing anyone else could do.

Communicating with the spirit took us marginally out of the world, into one of the twilight planes that fringe its borders. When we returned fully to our bodies time had passed. The big room was empty apart from ourselves and the wounded human. I hoped there'd been no fresh problems; we'd be busy with the healing for a while yet.

'What do you reckon?' my friend asked.

I shrugged.

'It wasn't as nasty as I expected,' I said. 'He's a strange human. I saw no lust for blood in him.'

'And his chances?'

I considered.

'Good,' I said. 'I see no physical reason why we can't heal him. But he has to hold on.'

There was the sound of gunshot from somewhere in the building. At the same time I felt a little ripple of force in the air.

'Someone just used power,' my friend said.

'The Sug,' I said. 'I thought he had none left.'

'So did I. It seems we thought wrong.'

My friend wanted fresh complications as little as I did. He looked at the closed door and sighed.

'It was him all right,' he said, 'but ... I trust him, much as it sticks in my craw to admit it. Whatever is going on, we'll sort it out later. The work here can't wait.'

He gave me one of his thin smiles.

'A Sug that I trust and a human worth trying to save,' he said. 'Surprises never end here, do they?'

He opened the dying monk's habit, exposing the bullet wound. Looking at it, I could almost understand the disgust humans roused in the Sug. What was one to make of a species that caused such damage so casually? They didn't even do it for food, and they did it without having any real evidence that the body's inhabitant had somewhere else to go.

'One crystal on the chest,' my friend said, 'and one on the back. There's no need for bandages – he won't move.'

The bleeding had already stopped. He held out his hand.

'Give me the stones,' he said.

I took them out of my pocket and gave them to him.

'Here goes nothing.'

33. Devils

Kirsten stared dumbly at the dead stranger on the floor. She seemed terribly calm.

'The ones who attacked us had no blood,' she said. 'This one certainly does.'

She looked at Simon.

'The patients,' she said. 'The crazy ones. Were any of them hurt when they were found? Were they bleeding?'

Simon had been looking in fascination at the frozen figure of Philip, who lay propped against the altar like an especially life-like dummy. At Kirsten's question he turned.

'What? No, none of them was injured – not physically anyway.'

Stephen didn't like being in the chapel anymore. The two immobile bodies were too strange.

'Let's get out of here,' he said.

Simon nodded.

'We'll go to the kitchen,' he said. 'I'll make some coffee or something.'

'What about the other strangers? Shouldn't we tell them what's happened.'

'They may already know. Let's just leave them to their work.'

In the hallway, Simon thought of something. He stopped short.

'You two go ahead,' he said. 'Put some water on to boil. I'd best reassure Thomas that he's not going to be slaughtered. He's locked himself in the television room.'

Kirsten was silent as they crossed the courtyard. She was too calm for Stephen's liking. It was as though she'd had one shock too many. In the kitchen he found a big kettle, filled it and put it on the range.

'Why are you interested in the blood?' he asked Kirsten.

'The ones with no blood seem to be the dangerous ones,' she said. 'The killers.'

'You're saying the big stranger was human?'

'I'm saying nothing about the others, really. I was wondering about *us*.'

He stared at her.

'You don't still think *we're* human, do you?' Kirsten asked.

Stephen's mouth opened to answer, but he could think of nothing to say. He didn't *feel* inhuman – but then, how could he be sure how that would feel?

Simon came in, shaking his head.

'It's incredible!' he said. 'Amazing!'

'What is?'

'I went to the television room. The door was wide open. And there was young Thomas, lying on the table, no less, sound asleep. I tried to wake him, but I couldn't.'

'That sounds like more of the strangers' work,' Kirsten said. 'I'm glad for Thomas, really – he was so frightened.'

'But that's not all. I went back to the chapel for a last look at Philip. I really quite like him like that, frozen. But the stranger, the dead one – he's gone!'

'*Gone?*'

'Gone! And so is his blood! It's as though he'd never been there at all!'

'But he was dead!' Kirsten said. 'He can't be gone! Has someone cleared up?'

Simon threw up his hands.

'We're not five minutes out of there,' he said. 'Besides, who is there to do it?'

Stephen was remembering the body in the field. It had been bloodless, and it had disappeared. Things still made no sense, but they were starting to fit into a pattern.

'There's still more,' Simon said. 'I thought I'd better check on the patients upstairs. But when I went up, guess what?'

'Don't tell me,' Stephen said. 'They're either gone or asleep.'

'Sleeping like babies, the lot of them. With big smiles on their faces – and that's as odd as anything else, I can assure you.'

The kettle began to boil. Simon rubbed his hands and started fetching coffee-making things from various cupboards. Stephen suspected that he was starting to enjoy all this in some strange way. When he said as much to Simon, the monk thought before answering.

'No,' he said. 'I'm enjoying the fact that it's nearly over. And I'm quite sure it is. I've felt it ever since those strangers arrived. They seem to know exactly what's going on. There's an air off them I like. They're …'

'Confident?' Stephen suggested.

'More than that. They're *professional*.'

'But professional *what*?' Stephen said. 'That's what I'd like to know.'

'Fix-it men,' Simon said. 'That's what they said.'

'They're not men, though, are they?' Kirsten asked in a quiet voice.

Simon stopped what he was doing and looked at her.

'No,' he said, 'I don't think they are. But I'm no Philip – the fact that they're strange to me doesn't mean I automatically think they're evil. These people don't seem to mean us any harm – quite the reverse, in fact. One of them has died for us, although admittedly death doesn't seem to mean much to them.'

'But if they hadn't come,' Stephen said, 'Philip wouldn't have gone over the edge. Paul wouldn't have been shot.'

Simon sighed.

'I've known Philip,' he said, 'ever since he came to our gates. I've never felt able to trust him. He has a thing in him that I saw a lot of after my own war. It's a mixture of guilt and self-pity, and it's a dangerous thing. He felt guilty about his past, but he couldn't take responsibility for it. It's eaten away at his insides for ten years now. All of this did something to him, of course, but Philip was already well on the way to some kind of madness. I've noticed him getting stranger for a long time. I tried to tell Paul that he didn't belong here, but Paul, being a good and a merciful man – a holy man, which I'm not – saw none of this. When this strangeness happened, I think Philip actually enjoyed it at first. He could be active and play with his guns like he always wanted to. He could try to forget the thing that was eating at him – the guilt.'

He frowned at them and shook his head, unable to explain himself fully.

'Some people,' he said, 'can't take responsibility for their own feelings. They need to find devils outside of themselves to blame their own guilt on. Of course there aren't any devils, so they invent them.'

By now the kettle was steaming. Simon went back to his coffee-making.

'You say those strangers drove Philip over the edge,' he said. 'But it wasn't their fault that he was so close to the edge to begin with. As we've agreed, they aren't human – how could they know how crazy humans are?'

'And us?' Kirsten's voice was small and fearful. 'What about us, Simon? Are *we* human?'

Again the old monk stopped and looked at her.

'I doubt it very much,' he said. 'But I wouldn't worry about it if I were you. What's so wonderful about being human?'

It was Kirsten's turn to struggle for words. Simon took pity on her.

'Humans can be wonderful creatures,' he said. 'But they rarely are – read your history books. For the most part we're worse than Philip's devils could ever be. We do evil to each other, evil to every species we encounter. Your … people, whatever they are, can't be much worse. They may even be better. It wouldn't be so very hard. Be careful, child. Naturally you're upset. But don't go looking for things to upset yourself further. I see nothing unnatural about either of you.'

'But you've admitted that we're not human!'

'Inhuman and unnatural are not the same thing at all. You're in the world, and there's nothing unnatural in the world.'

Before Kirsten could respond, footsteps sounded in the corridor outside. The three of them stared at the door.

The driver came in. He still wore his hat, but his jacket was draped over his arm and he'd loosened his collar and tie. His shirt was stuck to his skin with sweat. He looked completely drained. He walked to the table and sank into a chair.

'Do I smell coffee?' he asked in a weak voice.

Simon quickly poured a cup. The driver took it gratefully and drank deeply.

'Well?' Simon asked.

'He'll live, I think. The recovery has started, and my friend is supervising it. But it took a lot of effort, and I'm worn out. It's my second repair job today, remember.'

'Thank you,' Simon said. 'Thank you very much.'

'I'm glad we could help,' the driver said. 'After all, we're partly responsible for what happened.'

They told him about the events in the chapel. The driver nodded.

'I guessed it was something like that,' he said. 'I tidied up a bit, and I took the liberty of putting one of your people to sleep. I hope you don't mind.'

Simon positively chuckled.

'Mind?' he said. 'Not a bit.'

'And is it our turn now?' Kirsten asked.

The man's pale eyes looked at her.

'Not at all,' he said. He sighed again. 'I suppose I have some explaining to do.'

No one said anything to that. The driver looked directly at Simon, the eyes in his tired face weighing the old monk's reaction to his words.

'You'll have gathered,' he said, 'that we're not ... not quite like you.'

'No,' Simon said. 'You're not human.'

There it was.

'No. We're here to do a certain job. Until it's completed we can't leave – for your species's sake as well as our own. The job is almost done now, but there are a few loose ends – the creatures outside your walls, for instance.'

'Do they share your powers?' Simon asked.

'No. They're hunting things. They have no other purpose. But they're out of their owners's control. They're very dangerous, and yet – your human languages can't convey this very well – in some ways they're not even real, at least as you understand that word. Even to call them *creatures* is an exaggeration.'

'They're real enough to kill,' Kirsten said. Her voice was still harsh.

'Oh yes, they're real enough for that. But then it doesn't take very much reality to kill. Even shadows can kill, and in many ways that's all they are – shadows. When we destroy them, we don't even speak of 'killing' – we call it 'unshading'.'

With a shock, Stephen recalled the old man he'd seen in the courtyard that night. 'Unshade me,' the old man had pleaded with someone or something. Was he, then, a hunting thing as well?

'What about us?' Kirsten asked indicating herself and Stephen. 'Are *we* 'real'?'

The driver looked at her and smiled.

'Oh yes,' he said. 'You two are very real. Of course you are.'

'And the people upstairs?' Stephen asked.

'You mean the ones you call 'patients',' the driver said. 'You'll find this hard to accept, but there *are* no people upstairs. There never were. If you check them now you'll find that they are, in your terms, dead. They 'died' peacefully in their sleep.'

Simon bristled. His voice suddenly became cold, menacing.

'Are you telling me,' he said, 'that you've killed those poor unfortunate – what would you call them, non-people? *Untermensch*?'

His voice sneered the last word with disgust. The driver was shaking his head.

'No, no,' he said. 'You misunderstand. It's not a matter of opinion, I call them what they were. Certainly your 'patients' were *biologically* living. But they weren't *creatures*. All living creatures have what you would call a soul – the entities upstairs had none.'

Simon was confused.

'But if they weren't people,' he said, 'then what were they?'

The driver's face was a study in frustration as he tried to think of words to explain.

'You have no equivalent,' he said finally. 'Maybe you should think of them as a kind of video camera, or tape-recorder. Biological tape-recorders.'

'Biological tape-recorders,' Simon repeated blankly. There was a very long silence. The driver looked at each of them in turn, examining each face for some sign of comprehension. He saw none.

'I've heard all the stories about aliens from space,' Simon said eventually. 'I never dismissed them, but I never believed them either. I never had any proof one way or another. I suppose now I do. I've actually met creatures from another world.'

The effect of his words on the stranger was shocking. The driver's face paled, and he looked furious.

'Aliens from space?' he growled. 'I'll have you know I was born less than fifty miles from here! There isn't a human on this island more native to it than me!'

Simon blinked at him several times, taking in the man's obvious anger.

'Maybe,' he said, 'you should start at the beginning. Tell us the whole story.'

'Now that,' said the driver, calming down, 'is going to be hard for all of us.'

He was right. It was.

34. The Driver's Tale

'A long time ago,' the driver said, 'there were no humans on this island. You'll know this.'

'Of course,' said Simon. 'You're talking about, what, ten thousand years ago?'

'Give or take a few millennia, yes. My story begins then. The sea level was lower in those days. This island was already separated from the mainland, what you now call Europe, but the neighbouring island – Britain, you call it – was still connected to Europe by a narrow land-bridge that grew and shrank over time.

'There were, as I say, no humans here then, but the island was inhabited. It was home to two races which were … well, humanoid, as you'd say, but not human. Neither race was very numerous. There was much competition between them, but never anything like war. They couldn't have conceived of such a thing. They had less violent ways of competing.'

His eyes, which had been fixed on the table, flicked up at them as though to check whether they were listening. How he could have doubted it they didn't know.

'These races knew,' he continued, 'that both the neighbouring island and the mainland were inhabited, very sparsely, by other peoples. But they'd had little contact with them. The people here lived simple lives. They didn't go in for trade expeditions and such, because this land supplied all of their needs. And traders from outside tended to avoid this island, because other peoples thought the inhabitants were ... oh, monsters or witches, pick your own term of abuse. Your people have many words for such things, although none of them ever made much sense to me. At any rate, the people of this island lived here in peace, and they minded their own business.'

'Ah,' Simon said, 'whenever I hear of a peaceful people minding their own business I get a feeling something bad is coming.'

The driver nodded.

'Yes,' he said, 'it's the way, isn't it? Well, one fine day the island was invaded – just like that. No one had ever heard of such a thing before, so no one was prepared. Maybe we should have minded our own business a little bit less. If we had, we might have heard long before of the danger we faced.'

He looked around at them again.

'Some centuries before,' he said, 'a new people had begun to appear on the mainland. A very numerous people. They came streaming out of the east, out of the heartlands. Nothing like them had been seen before. They were primitive, tribal, warlike – actually, not to put too fine a point on it, they were complete savages. They killed without provocation, and they killed anything they met. They looted and despoiled, and when they had no one else to fight they fought amongst themselves. They easily conquered the few inhabitants of the coastal lands. And always more came, as though entire peoples had suddenly decided to move to a new land and kill everything in it.

'They hadn't even finished conquering the mainland when their first war-parties ventured over the land-bridge to the sister-island. There, the pattern repeated itself: contact, conflict, destruction. They ruined what land they took, and then they took more. They were a species which, by any known standards, was totally insane. It was as though they had no choice but to kill – as though they were machines programmed to destroy. And that was exactly what they did to every piece of land they conquered: they destroyed it, and everything in it.'

Stephen tried to imagine these grotesque, inhuman creatures. Could the hunting things that had attacked him and Kirsten in the library be some of them? Could they somehow have come here through time? Was that the cause of all this?

'Time passed,' the driver said. 'I'm speaking of centuries now, centuries upon centuries. The savages spread over the sister-island, killing everything they met. They grew in number and in organisation, and they grew smarter. But they grew no less savage. Eventually they came to the coast of the sister-island, and they realised that there was another land to the west. They decided to take that too.'

His listeners were glued to the driver's words. Simon had an odd distracted look on his face, as though he was thinking of something else at the same time that he was listening.

'I should tell you that one of the old races on this island was called – more or less – the Tellene,' the driver said. Stephen stiffened in his chair. The driver noticed. He looked Stephen in the eye as he went on.

'The second race,' he said, 'was called – and again it's an approximation – the Sug. They were a dull, unimaginative people, childish even – surly and given to tantrums and sulks. At least, that's how the Tellene saw them. To be fair, the Sug saw the Tellene as flighty and impractical. Too smart by half, as it were.'

'And the third race?' Simon asked sharply. 'The invaders? The savage species that killed and destroyed? The one *programmed* to kill and destroy?'

The driver said nothing. He raised his eyebrows briefly and looked embarrassed.

Simon's look was oddly intense. He seemed to find something terribly important in this puzzling story of a time before time.

'I know, don't I?' he said.

Again, the driver said nothing.

'Tell me,' Simon said. 'The killers were *us*, weren't they? They were humans!'

The driver seemed mortified.

'Well, yes,' he said regretfully. 'I'm afraid they were.'

35. Agent On the Job

The noontime sun was bright in the courtyard when I went outside. The air was fat and drowsy with riches of bee-song and flowers. I drank it in.

The healing process in the abbot's body had begun. It was simply a matter of time now, and out of my hands. Sometimes nothing is the most useful thing you can do. And there was another little matter to clear up before we left.

I crossed to the monastery gates and looked out. Through the screen of trees I could see the sunshine glittering on the waters of the sacred lake. The air was full of the smell of the green growing things, and of the thing that no human could feel: the place's nature. Humans didn't even have words to describe that smell – a smell of wholeness, and of something more than wholeness – a smell of *potential*. They'd obviously noticed something special about this spot, otherwise they'd never have built here in the first place. But they didn't have the senses to know what that something special was.

The place's personality had helped to heal my own wound, and it was helping the healing of the wounded monk. But it would be hurting the killing things that lurked out there now among the trees.

No real power has any owner except itself — it has only those by whom it consents to be used. This place had never been ours; but it was a source for the power we used. It had been our ally, because we'd respected it and roused it from its first, unthinking sleep. We'd revealed it to itself. We'd told it what it was. 'Look at yourself,' we'd said. 'Are you not beautiful?' Since our going the power had slept. Now it was starting to wake itself, for reasons that we couldn't know. But when it was ready, it would tell us — that was power's way.

The crystal stones were still in the refectory, channelling energy to the abbot's dreaming flesh. But I'd be fine without them. I strolled down the gravel path from the gates. Around me in the greenery birds fluttered and called, but in a place quite near I sensed the silence of their absence.

That would be the place.

I sent a call there, bidding the killing things to come. They didn't move. I called them more sharply, ordering now. They came silently, nervous, from between young green branches, and stood huddled in front of me. Their shoulders were slumped, their whole stance subdued — the place terrified them. They reminded me of the humans of my parents' day, that first killing brood whose fear was almost as strong as their bloodlust. But with these things fear had the upper hand. They were weary of this unfriendly world. They were dirty and ragged and mixed-up and mad, four boys with the too-lean look of famished hunting dogs.

'Your masters didn't mean to do this to you,' I told them. 'They made a mistake. But the game is over now. You can have peace.'

One of them looked up at me. His mouth hung slack. There was a big bruise on his cheek. One of his eyes was swollen shut. In the other eye I saw a dull spark of half-understanding.

'Peace?' he said. His untrained mouth mangled the word.

I felt angry at the Sug. It was cruel to make such unfinished things. And yet the Sug were not cruel as such, only thoughtless, which can be worse than any cruelty.

'Peace,' I said again.

It wasn't the word they understood so much as the tone. To my surprise, I felt pity for them. These killing things had been made to suit a purer version of this world. The humans had polluted its air, which even humanity itself knew now; but as yet they had no way of sensing what they'd done to the world's subtler air. If they did find a way to measure it, it would probably be with a machine – humans have always loved their toys.

The Sug could have known better than to make this mess, but they'd been too busy sulking. Their pride had left their creatures to this miserable agony in a fouled world. Still, the Sug who'd died today had behaved in a way no Tellene could have expected. The exquisite manners of his gesture would have made any of the Tellene proud. The world was full of surprises – it was one of the things my people liked most about it.

'Come,' I said to the hunters. 'Let's end this nonsense.'

The one who'd tried to speak came forward first. There was a light in his eyes like something you'd see in the eyes of a trusting young animal. He bent his head as I raised my arm, and he bared his thin neck to my hand. The others jostled for places in the queue.

When it was done I stood for a while in the shade of the green trees, listening to the singing of the birds. My friend, I presumed, was with the others. I guessed he was explaining things to them, and I wondered what lies he was telling.

36. The Third Alternative

Simon was quiet for a time. He seemed to have forgotten all of them. Then his eyes turned back to the driver.

'Where,' he asked carefully, 'does this story lead?'

The driver tapped the table in front of him.

'Here,' he said. 'To this place. To this moment. To here and to now.'

Simon gave a short nod.

'And why are you telling it to me? Why not just send me to sleep, like the others?'

The driver smiled.

'I'm afraid the narration isn't really for your benefit, Brother Simon,' he said. 'It's for the other two. But I must admit, I feel a certain relief telling it to a human – our races have never exactly *communicated*. And to tell the truth, it doesn't matter if you hear it.'

'No?'

'No. Because after we leave nobody in this monastery will remember we've been here. They'll remember none of this. Your people outside will be left with a mystery, but no more. Even that much is regrettable – but we can't make your whole species forget that part of this island became inaccessible for nearly a week. Even we're not *that* good.'

'Ha!' said Simon, slapping the table. He didn't seem terribly put out. To Stephen's surprise he was actually smiling, and there was something like pleasure in his voice.

'You know,' he said, 'I really could admire you people. You have style. You come, you do your job and you go – no messing around.'

The driver nodded acknowledgement of the compliment.

'Do you still want to hear the rest?' he asked.

'Of course! You can't stop now!'

The driver shrugged, and resumed his story.

'As I've said, the old peoples minded their own business. They knew nothing of what had been happening elsewhere. So when a fleet of primitive boats turned up and landed strangers on their shores, they were surprised. Actually, it was hard to know who was *more* surprised – the invaded or the invaders. Because the native races were, as I've told you, humanoid, but not human – they didn't *look* like you. And when the newcomers looked at them, they seemed to see–'

'Monsters?'

'Yes. Monsters.'

The driver's cup had been empty for some time. Now he asked politely for a refill. Kirsten, who'd been listening as closely as the others, jumped up and poured. The driver took a long drink before continuing.

'You can't understand what came next unless you know a few things about the old races,' he said. 'For one thing, they were very advanced for their time. For another, they absolutely loathed senseless violence. It wasn't that they were cowardly – far from it. But they knew that violence, like any powerful tool, could be very dangerous for the user. Violence *taints* the user. It damages his spirit to the exact degree that it is used.'

Simon made a wordless little noise of agreement. He looked even more closely at the driver.

'Another fact about the native races was that, after a fashion, their reputation as witches was earned. They had powers that would seem magical – unnatural – to humans even now. In fact, they were simply more aware of what nature allowed, and nature allows a very great deal more than humans care to know.

'It was obvious from the first that the newcomers were invaders, not traders or anything else. And it was obvious too that they were … unpleasant. Their boats were decorated with human heads and hands. When they landed they sacrificed other humans on the shore, thanking their cruel gods for a safe journey. These sacrifices involved extreme pain for the victims, which the newcomers obviously enjoyed inflicting. But the old races didn't need to see these things to understand the newcomers. You see, they could … well, you'd say they could read minds.

'The invading force was large, but in itself this wouldn't have been a problem for the natives. They were few in number, but compared to the savages they were very powerful. Their weapons weren't physical ones, but still they could have exterminated the invaders if they'd been so inclined.

'The problem was that they *weren't* so inclined. Violence on that level just wasn't their way. They found it distasteful as well as dangerous. Manners were extremely important in their society, and they found such violence *ill-mannered*.'

Simon interrupted.

'But you said the invaders thought they were monsters,' he said. 'Weren't they afraid to attack them?'

'Fear did seem to be the second strongest emotion they had – they feared everything. But the fear gave rise to something else, which was by far the strongest emotion they knew: hatred. They hated what they didn't understand. And they understood very little.'

Again Simon nodded agreement.

'Yes,' he said. 'Yes. And they haven't changed much, have they?'

'Oh, but they've changed a great deal. In those days all of your race was like that all of the time – fearful and murderous, and little else.'

'So what did the natives here do?'

'The invaders attacked. The natives defended. They erected barriers to contain the strangers – barriers a bit like the one we've put up now, but much more primitive.'

Simon gave a bitter little laugh.

'*The strangers*,' he repeated. 'That's what *we*'ve been calling *you*! Why don't you call them by their name: humans?'

'Very well. I was only being polite. The natives contained the humans while they decided what to do. This took a long time. The Sug and thTellene set out to discover who these people were. When they found out – from the minds of the humans themselves – they were horrified that such brutes could exist. The Sug in particular were appalled. They sugg-ested that this species must be some awful mistake, that it wasn't just our business, but our *duty* to annihilate them all, here and wherever they lived – to restore balance to the world.'

'That's a dangerous way of thinking,' Simon muttered.

'Indeed. That's what the Tellene said. You must understand that these things weren't moral questions for us, just simple logic: if you cut your hand, you bleed; if you kill, you take on the responsibility of a killer. Killing a whole species involves an enormous level of responsibility, even if that species seems to be truly vermin. But the Tellene had seen that these *creatures* – these humans – would simply keep coming back. It wasn't a matter of choice for them – they were *driven* things. Eventually it would have come to violence anyway. If we destroyed them, then we'd become just like them. But if we didn't destroy them, and if they kept coming, then eventually they'd swamp us through sheer numbers – we were, as I've told you, quite few. In either case we would be, in our own eyes, destroyed, whether in a thousand years or in a day. In many ways a day would be preferable: if we kept them at bay for a thousand years through blood and slaughter, then by the end of that time we ourselves would be brutalised beyond our own recognition, just as if we'd annihilated them in the first place. We'd be – if you don't mind my saying so – no better than humans.'

'But what choice do you have in these situations?' Simon said. You could see he was taking the question personally, and that it was one he'd thought about before. 'It's the old debate: resistance or destruction, when resistance may lead to your own *moral* destruction, the destruction of the very things you want to defend.'

'Yes,' the driver said. 'I see you understand me very well.'

Simon seemed agitated.

'But surely in the end there is no choice,' he said. 'You can personally decide that you'd rather die than kill. That's your right. But what about your friends, your children, your whole society – all you believe in! Can you stand by and watch them be destroyed without lifting your hand? Is that principle, or just cowardice?'

His voice rose as he spoke.

'That's a human question,' the driver said. 'Faced with such a situation, humans have those two options: resist or don't resist. The Tellene realised that they and the Sug had a third alternative.'

'A *third*?'

'A third. The Tellene thought long and hard about such choices as they had. You must understand that they tended to take the long view of things. Both of the old races were long-lived – very much so in your terms. But the Tellene regarded the Sug as hasty – which they still are. They tend to act without thinking of the consequences, which is why we're all sitting here in the first place. The Tellene, on the other hand, have always tended to think in longer terms.'

'Longer than centuries?'

'Oh dear, yes. Much longer.'

'Millennia?'

'When they're in a hurry they might think in terms of mill-ennia. But they'd regard it as short-term thinking, and they wouldn't be entirely comfortable with it.'

Simon took a while to digest that. But he was caught up in the driver's story.

'So tell me,' he said. 'What did the Tellene suggest?'

'They suggested that both races abandon the island to the newcomers.'

'Just like that?'

'Just like that.'

'And go where? America?'

'Dear me, no! The Tellene realised that in time these new creatures would spread all over the planet – their urges were just too strong. Going to another place would only postpone the problem. And then this island was our home, and we are attached to our home in a way humans can't understand. So the Tellene suggested that they and the Sug go …'

The driver looked at the old monk, weighing up his possi-ble reaction. Then he gave one of his shrugs and told him.

'Nowhere,' he said. 'They suggested that they and the Sug abandon this world completely and live, without bodies, in another place they knew – though 'place' is the wrong word. This 'place', you see, isn't a place at all. It isn't anything. Your languages can't describe it, because your minds can't con-ceive it. It has neither time nor space. It has nothing. And that's what we call it: Noplace, or Nowhere. Because that's what it is.'

Simon looked blankly at the slight man in front of him. Stephen and Kirsten, who'd been hanging on the driver's every word, looked just as blankly at each other.

'Nowhere,' Simon said.

'Nowhere.'

Simon gave a long, long sigh.

'Well,' he said. 'I suppose I did ask you to explain. Now could you please do something else for me?'

'But of course. What?'

'Could you please explain the explanation?'

37. Into Nowhere

While they waited for the driver to go on, Stephen thought of what the man had said already. He was trying to find some echo of recognition in the story. If he was a Tellene – and that seemed to be the case – then surely he must know this story. But none of it sounded familiar at all.

He looked at Kirsten. Like Simon, she was watching the driver. The look on her face was impossible to read. Stephen wanted to go outside with her, to ask her what she thought. But then the driver started speaking again.

'This is the hardest part of the story to tell,' he said. 'Or at least, the hardest part for you to understand. I need to ask you something before I start. Tell me, what is a soul?'

Simon was taken aback.

'A soul?' he repeated. 'Why ... well, in the broadest terms, our religions see it as the non-physical part of a person. It's in the body but not really of it. The body is its container, as it were.'

'All right,' the driver said. 'I won't use the word, because it has religious overtones for humans that it doesn't have for us. But remember what you've said: *the body as a container for a spirit.*

'Now, neither the Tellene nor the Sug had anything you

would recognise as a religion. They didn't really need one. They had direct experience of many things your various religions can only guess at. I'm not talking about beliefs, they didn't have beliefs – they had *knowledge*.'

He rapped the table in front of him with his knuckles.

'You wouldn't say you *believed* in this table,' he said. 'It would be a pointless statement. You just know it's there. The old people had direct experience of what humans might call other ... dimensions, I suppose. Other spheres of being. Again, your languages don't have proper words for these things. The old people viewed their bodies as containers, as forms worn by their spirits in this particular sphere. In other spheres, with other physical laws, the spirits needed other containers. I say again, this wasn't a matter of belief, it was a matter of everyday experience, just as this table is to you. The old people travelled in those spheres in a way just as real as any journey in this one. Are you still with me?'

'Was I ever?' Simon asked. Then he nodded. 'I think so,' he said.

'I can't describe these other places to you. All of your human languages are based on your experience of this world. The other worlds are not like this one, they have their own languages to describe them.'

'And the Tellene suggested that they and the Sug should go to one of these ... other worlds?' Simon asked.

'No. That wasn't possible. Other worlds are only suitable for visits. We could visit those places, but we weren't native to them – *this* is our world. You can't really understand, but if you stay in another world long enough, you become a creature of it – you *belong* there – and you can't go back to your own world permanently. But you do stay attached to your own world, whose child, after all, you originally are. You're torn between the two. This is extremely painful. The closest I can come to it in human terms is to call it a kind of *homesickness*. But, for our people, a killing kind.'

'And so no alternative at all,' Simon said.

'No. But luckily this wasn't all that there was. You could think of these places – these worlds – as stations on a railway line. But there was another place we knew, and it was – in those terms – like a junction on that line. A big junction. It wasn't a place like any other. In fact it wasn't a place at all. It was ... *between* places. There was no matter at all there – strictly speaking, there was no 'there' there for any matter to be in. No space. No time. Nothing except – when you went 'there', and in a very unusual way – yourself. And because it wasn't really a place, you could never become a creature of that place – that Noplace. What the Tellene suggested was that, instead of perishing physically or morally, they and the Sug should go into exile in the Noplace.'

There had been several points in the driver's narrative where the only adequate response was silence. The silences had grown deeper. This was the deepest of all. It was Simon who broke it.

'But why? What could you do there?'

'We could *wait*,' the driver said.

'Wait? Wait for what?'

The driver said nothing, only looked at him with his pale bland eyes. Understanding slowly dawned on Simon's face.

'You thought we'd destroy ourselves, didn't you?' he said.

'It did seem likely, yes. There was a chance your species might become civilised in time, but it didn't seem like much of a chance. Eventually, humans would run out of places to go and creatures to kill. They'd use up the resources they needed and they'd fall to self-destruction. If they didn't destroy themselves completely then at least they'd damage themselves so much that they would no longer pose a threat. Then we could come back and pick up the pieces. We saw going to Nowhere as being like climbing a hill when there's a flood – when the waters recede, you come back down. All you need to do is wait. And in the Noplace, of course, there's no time, so there's no waiting as such.'

'So you went,' Simon said. 'You all went.'

'Yes. We went.'

'But if there's no time in this place then … when you say "we" you mean it literally, don't you? You were there, you personally! You're ten thousand years old!'

'Not really. I've spent most of it outside time. But I was here that long ago, yes.'

'And your body …'

'Was made yesterday, and when my job is over it will return to nothing, to the dust it was made of.'

Simon kept shaking his head, more in shock than disbelief.

'And you all stayed outside time until now?' he said.

'Oh no. We send people back. We assume human form and

we return. Mostly it's enough to send creatures such as your 'patients'. But sometimes we find it necessary to come ourselves. And that, I'm afraid, leads to more trouble for you. Because what I've told you so far doesn't explain why the four of us are sitting here now.'

Simon fixed him with a bleary eye.

'You mean there's *more*?'

'I'm afraid so.'

Simon sighed for what seemed like the hundredth time.

'I'm beginning to feel sorry that I asked for an explanation in the first place,' he said.

'Then maybe I should stop. You've heard as much as you want to.'

Simon's laugh was almost sarcastic.

'Oh no,' he said. 'In some ways I've heard much *more* than I want to. But now that you've started, I want it all.'

'Even though you'll forget?'

'Even so.'

This time the driver went over and refilled his coffee cup himself.

'Very well, Brother Simon,' he said. 'Now this is where it all gets a bit *strange*.'

This time Simon's laugh was very sarcastic indeed.

38. An Agent Reflects

The human's chest rose and fell with the rhythm of his breathing. It was almost normal now. The chest wound was still a little raw on the outside, but that was fading as I watched. In a little while there wouldn't even be a bruise. Once begun, the work had gone quickly. The flesh had slept and dreamed about a time before its rupture, and the stones had helped it to make its dreaming real. It was all they ever did, really.

I'd been so pleased with the result that I'd taken the process a step beyond what was necessary. The abbot's body had been in good condition before the wound, but it had been the well-preserved body of a middle-aged man. Now, while his flesh dreamed and remembered, I'd prompted its memory to go back a bit further. When the process was finished the abbot's inner organs would be as they'd been when he was half his present age. So long as he took care to avoid further bullets and such, he'd live well beyond the time set for him. If you're going to interfere at all, I reckoned, then you might as well go all the way.

It was bright outside, but in the refectory there was a kind of dusk. Shafts of light fell through high narrow windows. I looked at the dust-motes floating in the light and thought about our visit. We'd done well, I thought, in difficult circumstances. Catastrophe had been avoided. Our people had been rescued. Security had been maintained. The humans inside the barrier would forget us; those outside would be left with a puzzle. That might even be good for them.

We too, though, had our puzzles to consider as a result of the mission. It had been a downright peculiar affair: Sugs acting decently; humans acting sanely – it was all a bit of a revelation to me. Live and learn, as my mother always advised me. I hoped she'd be all right now. I'd done my best.

I thought of the restless stirrings of power that were coming from the lake. There was no way to know what they meant, but they had to mean something. And then the fact that these monks were here at all – that meant our power had failed here in the old sacred place. That was a first, and it too must mean something. But there was no point in wondering about any of it – when the right time came, we'd see what we'd see.

In my mind I ran over the things that still needed to be done. I'd overlooked nothing I could think of. The novice was asleep. The big Irish monk was frozen where the Sug had left him. I'd looked in his mind, and what I'd found there hadn't been pretty. There was an old guilt there, and an old hatred. It had stewed away inside him for years. It had helped cause his loss of control now. The monk himself was appalled by it, but he was too far gone to control it. So I'd fixed it myself, taking the guilt. It seemed easier, somehow, now that I'd already worked on one human. They were simple creatures, really, their problems so basic that they were quite easy to help.

The bodies of the 'dead' would dissolve into nothing now that they had been switched off. The Sug's body was already gone. Only our own flesh remained to be vacated, but we couldn't do that just yet. We'd have to clear away every sign of our presence before we left. The rooms used, the utensils, everything would have to be minutely checked. The human authorities would be all over this place once we removed the barrier.

It was hard to believe that everything had gone so smoothly. There had been no major difficulties. It didn't seem quite natural. Chance is chance, but many things that pass for chance are nothing of the kind. I felt the clean air around me, the hard grain of purity in it that even all these years of humanity hadn't managed to tarnish. The oddities had some-thing to do with the place, I was certain of that. There had been rare energies let loose around here lately, and not all of them were ours. It wasn't for me to guess at their cause or effect. Even after we'd gone, the place wouldn't be the same again. It would be noticed by any creature with any kind of sensitivity at all – a subtle difference in atmosphere for which they'd have no name.

Looking around the room, I caught a glint of movement from the corner of my eye. When I turned to look, I saw my own reflection looking back at me from the glass door of a tall cupboard by the wall. I walked over and stood in front of it, just looking. A dark-haired bare-chested man looked calmly back at me. We were in two worlds that reflected each other, separated by a fragile shining screen. One world had substance, the other did not. Which was which? We fingered the bandages on our necks. Beneath mine, the flesh felt whole. I unwound the long linen strip and my double did the same with his. Better. I turned my head this way and that, examining the neck. There was a faint line where the join had been. The neat lines of the stitching were clearly visible. I cut the thread with my nails, took one end and slowly pulled. It came out cleanly and easily, with an odd but not unpleasant *pulling* sensation. I put the thread in my back pocket and looked at the neck again. It was fine. It seemed a pity I'd be losing it so soon. I left my reflection to go about his business, and went back for a last look at the abbot.

The colour was returning to the tall monk's face. A long lean face, a face with character. I raised him carefully to look at the exit wound in his back. It wasn't there anymore. I had to smile. Perfect healing, and of a human. The real miracle was that he hadn't died of shock when he was shot: staying alive then had been something he'd done for himself. A strong man.

I stood up and stretched. I took a last look at my reflection in the glass across the room. The ghost man in the glass stood looking back at me evenly. I raised my hand to him. He raised his in reply.

'So long, man,' I said.

His lips moved, but I heard nothing, only my own footsteps echoing back from the stone walls as I walked out of that cool stone room forever.

39. The Matter In Hand

'Nowhere is hard to describe,' the driver said. 'In fact, it's impossible. No time, no space, no matter – there's nothing *to* describe. For our spirits, there's less individuality than we're used to; yet in some ways, there's much more. After we'd been there for a while we began to realise how limited our ideas had been when we lived in this world. You think quite differently when you've no body, you know.'

'I daresay you do,' Simon said dryly.

'We learned, for instance, the true degree to which matter is – how can I put it – a *shadow*. A shadow of thought, of spirit. I'm not talking now in any religious sense, far from it. Maybe this makes no sense to you.'

Simon was still staring at him.

'But it does,' he said. 'It's a basic part of many human philosophies. There was a man called Plato who had a famous parable about it.'

'But I don't mean a parable. I mean a simple *fact*. Back here we found that the new ideas we'd learned in the Noplace gave us a different relationship with *this* world. We'd always been powerful here by human standards. Now we were more so. Not that we'd learned any special thing – it's just that we now *thought* of things differently. Look here.'

He casually put his hand through the table top. There were three sharp intakes of breath.

'A simple parlour trick,' the driver said. 'Sleight of hand. Any one of you could do it very easily – except for the fact that you know it's impossible. I couldn't have done that so easily before going to the Noplace, and I can't say that I ever *learned* to do it. But once, when I was back here, it simply struck me that there was no reason why I couldn't.'

'Can you appear in two places at once?' Stephen asked.

'Of course. Under some circumstances it just happens – when someone close to me is in some kind of danger, for instance.'

He chuckled.

'Don't humans talk about being "beside yourself with worry"? Well, this is the same thing – only you're not beside yourself, you're a bit further away.'

He drew his hand out of the table, but Simon's eyes stayed fixed on the place where it had gone in.

'But why?' the old monk muttered. 'Why do you bother coming back at all?'

For the first time since his arrival, the driver looked a little nonplussed.

'We have our own needs, you know,' he said. 'For one thing, we starve. Not for physical food, of course. But your spirit can starve too. We're creatures of the senses, like all born to flesh. We starve for sight and sound and touch. We starve for the simple fleshly experience of our lost home. We do send our creatures back – creatures like your 'patients'. They collect ... *sensations*. Words won't describe it. I've called these creatures biological tape-recorders. When – to use that metaphor – the tape is full, we take them back. Then we play the tape and *share* the sensations. We can *drink* their experiences just like I can drink this coffee, and our spirits gain sustenance and nourishment from it. We can all share in it. Imagine if, say, humans could actually *feed* on music, a whole hall full of you feeding on the notes of a symphony.'

Simon's eyes had taken on a slightly glazed look.

'The Sug, now,' the driver said, 'they'll have none of this. Going to Nowhere seems to have used up what little common sense they had. They did send their own people back at first, but they soon sickened of being among humans. So they stopped coming. They now prefer to recycle old sensations and memories – and so, of course, they've lost touch completely with the reality of this world. They'd rather blame the Tellene for persuading them to leave it in the first place – as I've said, they sulk.

'It's hard for the Tellene to be among humans, too. But we accept reality, we learn to bear it . To us, the world itself is the important thing. But the Sug still regret not having their way in the first place. They suspect that they made a mistake in letting the Tellene persuade them to go. So they resent the Tellene, and when they *do* come back – which hasn't happened for thousands of years – they spend their time trying to interfere with Tellene operations here. As I said, the old races competed – to you their conflicts would seem like complicated games of one-upmanship. The Tellene felt it was past time for such games, but the Sug still work out their resentment in the same old way. It's childish, but there you are – the Sug are a childish people.'

'That man who saved us in the chapel,' Kirsten said, 'was he a Sug?'

'He was. A most unusual one.'

'So they came back now. For the first time in millennia. Why?'

The driver smiled.

'You're a smart girl,' he said.

We're reaching the nub of it now, Stephen thought. We're reaching our part. And I'm not sure I want to know about it at all.

The driver looked at him.

'I'm sorry if this frightens you,' he said, 'but facts are facts.'

He looked around at all of them.

'We who made the original journey,' he said, 'had actual memories of this world. We'd grown up here. But we were few, as I've told you. And the Noplace has no physical things there at all – nothing. So we needed to come back here to have our children. And once those children were born, we didn't want to feed their minds on second-hand sensations, as the Sug did. That's a very dangerous thing to do to young creatures. It makes for incomplete people – I'm speaking quite literally. We wanted our children to have *actual* experience of the world we loved. We wanted them to have *lives*.'

Simon drew a sharp breath.

'Your children grow up here!' he said. 'They grow up as ...'

'As humans. Yes.'

Both of them turned now to look at Stephen and Kirsten. In Simon's wide eyes there was something almost like awe. The driver's eyes had dropped their bland mask. There was open fondness in his look now. Kirsten and Stephen looked back at them with identical expressions of numbness.

'So I'm ... a Tellene,' Stephen said. 'A Tellene who's grown up as a human?'

'And me?' said Kirsten. 'Me too?'

'You are. And very special ones. This may be the hardest part for you to accept, but ...'

He paused.

'Yes?' Both Kirsten and Stephen said at the same time.

'Well, the Tellene weren't a tribal people. They weren't what you call a democracy either. The closest thing humans would have to our society would be a kind of monarchy.'

'They—' Kirsten began, then stopped. She frowned, trying to work out what he was implying.

Simon began, very gently, to chuckle. Stephen and Kirsten stared at him, bewildered. Gradually the chuckle broadened into a hearty laugh. Simon slapped his knee.

'My dear children,' he said, 'I think what our friend here is saying is that you two are royalty.'

If Kirsten's face had looked blank before, now it looked positively uninhabited.

'You ...' she said, whirling to look at Stephen. 'I ...'

Stephen was no help. The absence of expression on her face was mirrored on his own.

'But this is plain mad!' he said

Now Kirsten laughed too. There was a hint of hysteria in it.

'No, it's not,' she said. 'It's a fairytale!'

The driver smiled.

'It just goes to show you,' he said. 'It's a funny old world.'

40. The Real Adventure

Kirsten couldn't stop laughing. She'd subsided to a giggle, but it went on and on.

'I'm a princess!' she said. 'Me! A princess! That's ridiculous!'

Simon seemed to be lost in his own thoughts. From the look on his face they were difficult ones.

'Do you know,' he said to the driver, 'you can't imagine how interesting I've found your story. It tied up with all sorts of things I've thought about for more than fifty years now. That's nothing to you, I know, but to us it's a very long time.'

'Are you sorry you'll forget the tale, then?'

'No, I'm not. Because it disturbed me too. People say I have a dim view of my own species. But it turns out that maybe I've been overestimating it.'

'All creatures have childhoods,' the driver said. 'All species too. And children are not always wise – how could they be? They're new things under the sun. But adults have no such excuse.'

'Tell me one thing,' Simon said, 'do the Tellene have a god?'

The driver looked puzzled.

'I have to admit,' he said, 'I've never really understood that particular human idea. If I have a god – in so far as I understand the word – then you could say my god is information. It's here all around you – in the table and the chairs, in the grass and the sky. But your species doesn't seem to care much for information. Half the time you don't even notice it. I know you have notions of what you call 'heaven'. In fact, some of those notions make 'heaven' sound more than a little like Nowhere. But to us heaven is *here* – in this world full of wonders. Heaven is *now*. And you humans control it, or you think you do, but you don't seem to *care* for it much. We find that … *odd*.'

'Odd, yes. That's one word for it.'

Simon looked with narrowed eyes at the affable other.

'You must hate us very much,' he said. 'We took your whole world. Literally. How you must long for our destruction!'

'Not at all! That would be foolish. You are children of this world, as we all are. What you do with yourselves is your business. Long ago you interfered with us. We chose our response, and there it ended. We live with reality, not dreams. We're a practical people.'

'That you are, my friend. That you certainly are.'

'But I still don't know what happened to us!' Stephen complained. 'Why is all this happening *now*?'

'It has something to do with those Sug creatures,' Kirsten said.

'Indeed,' the driver said. 'Things like this usually do. You two have been here since your birth. You were due to ... to come *home*, for want of a better word. Not a real home, but all we have. Our halting site. Some of our creatures were due to come back with you – we call them creatures, even though they're alive only in the broadest sense of that word. We send such creatures often – far more often than we come ourselves. They stay here awhile and they just ... have experiences. They live as humans, they take jobs, sometimes they marry – they do all the things that humans do. Nobody here notices.

'The Sug seem to have concluded at some point that sending our young and our creatures here was giving us some kind of advantage over them. Don't ask me how they came to that conclusion, I don't pretend to understand their minds. Maybe they were just bored – it can't be a very interesting existence when you do nothing but sulk. At any rate, they thought they'd interfere with this particular operation. It was meant to be a sort of game – as I've told you, we have always competed through something like one-upmanship.

'The Sug decided to ruin the homecoming of our most important children – you two. They sent an agent with a hunting pack of their own creatures to attack you and destroy your companions. You came to these mountains, which had always been important to us. Just as you prepared to leave, your party was ambushed – not physically, but effectively. A psychic attack humans would call it. Your own minds were confused, those of your creature companions were ... destroyed, really. Completely short-circuited. But the Sug operation went wrong. Disastrously wrong. They'd miscalculated badly.

They'd stayed away too long, so they had no idea how much the atmosphere here had been changed by humans in the millennia since they'd last been here. The non-physical atmosphere, I mean.'

'The non-physical atmosphere,' Simon repeated, shaking his head with a bewildered air.

'Yes. It's as real to us as the physical one and, if anything, your species has polluted it even more. The Sug agent was damaged as soon as he arrived. The creatures they'd sent were outmoded – old models unsuited to this time. In the middle of their assault they went berserk, and turned on the agent when he showed up. It was the spiritual air that did it.'

'The spiritual air,' Simon muttered, shaking his head. But there was humour as well as bewilderment in his tone.

'It was a very dangerous situation,' the driver said. 'The Sug creatures were hunters and they were out of control, that made them very, very dangerous – for humans, too. It was as though some of your own ancestors had arrived back here among you. Dyed-in-the-wool killers, knowing no sanity at all. We knew at once that there was something wrong. So we sealed the area and cleared it.'

'You cleared it,' Simon said. 'Just like that.'

'Yes. Just like that. We'd never done such a thing before, not since we'd left, but it proved to be simple enough. But we couldn't find our missing people by our normal means – so we had to come in person. Outside the barrier your human authorities are going frantic, but there's no way they can get in. We really didn't want to do such a thing – it's a bit *show-offish* for our taste. Flashy, you know? But we couldn't take any risks with the Sug creatures – they were just too dangerous.'

'You didn't clear us,' Simon said. 'Why?'

'I honestly don't know. Maybe in our hurry we overlooked you.'

Simon looked at him with some disbelief, but before he could say anything Stephen interrupted.

'What I don't understand,' he said, 'is why you ... why *we* stay in this Nowhere *now*. Maybe humanity was savage once. But surely not nowadays. The Tellene could contact the United Nations, or–'

He stopped. All three were looking at him sceptically.

'That would be madness,' Simon said. 'There are too many Philips in the world, liable to turn savage in the face of anything they don't understand. Too many savages under the skin. And a lot of them are in positions of power, not buried in some mountain monastery.'

'Yes,' the driver said. 'I must admit this Philip did rouse a kind of sad nostalgia in me. I've seen many like him among your people in my time.'

Stephen blushed. He could see his own foolishness when it was pointed out to him.

'So, what now?' Kirsten asked.

'Well,' the driver said, 'my friend will have been clearing up. The various bodies have dissolved.'

'It's funny,' Simon said. 'All this violence, and then you tell me nobody really died at all – apart from that man, that ... Sug in the chapel. And from what you say, his death didn't matter very much to him.'

'Not at all. It was less than an inconvenience.'

'Less than an inconvenience,' Simon said. 'Yes. I see.'

Again he shook his head.

'I think,' he said gravely, 'that I need some fresh air. I'm going out to the courtyard for a while. To think about your story.'

And without looking back, he went out. He looked like a man who was weighed down with a great many thoughts. Stephen watched him as he went.

'He's bewildered,' he said. 'So am I.'

Light footsteps sounded in the corridor. The second Tellene came in. He had put his shirt and jacket on, and was knotting his thin knitted tie. He smiled at them broadly.

'I see you've been telling Brother Simon a story,' he said to his friend. 'I could tell by the expression on his face. Or maybe I should say the absence of one.'

The driver chuckled.

'He's a good man,' he said. 'Have you tidied up?'

'Yes. We're all clear.'

'And the abbot?'

'As good as new. Better, in fact.'

The driver looked at Stephen and Kirsten.

'Well, folks,' he said, 'we've a car to leave back at a house, and then we can go. Are you ready?'

'Not really,' Stephen said. 'But as ready as I'll ever be.'

'*I'm* ready,' Kirsten said, 'this is going to be the *real* adventure!'

Her eyes were shining. It's not every day, Stephen supposed, that you find out you're a princess – even if it's the princess of Nowhere.

The driver took his cup over to a sink and rinsed it. He upturned it and put it carefully down on the wooden drying rack.

'Let's go so,' he said.

So they did.

PART FOUR: These Our Actors

41. Family Reunions

In the fading afternoon light a dusty car drove down an unkempt country road. In the front seat were two ordinary-looking men in dark suits, in the back seat a boy and a girl. They'd been driving for some time in silence, each lost in their own thoughts. Though not all of them knew it, each in their own way was thinking about exactly the same thing: the events of the previous days in this part of the world.

Stephen wasn't comfortable in his mind. The long explanation he'd heard had raised at least as many questions as it had answered, and they were all questions he badly wanted to ask. But he didn't know where to start or, in some cases, how to ask at all.

He looked at Kirsten, who had a dreamy smile on her face. Still pleased at the notion of being a princess, he supposed. The Princess of Nowhere. And as for himself … he leaned forward suddenly and spoke to the men in the front seat.

'Here,' he said, 'if Kirsten is a princess, does that mean that she and I are … does that make me …'

But he didn't know how to go on. Both men smiled.

'A prince?' said the younger one.

'Well, yes, I suppose so. Is that what I am?'

The two men exchanged a meaningful glance.

'Not exactly,' the driver said. 'You'll understand in a little while.'

'But I want to know *now*.'

The younger man sniggered. The older one laughed outright. Stephen was annoyed. What had he said?

'Look,' the driver said patiently. 'I told Brother Simon what I felt he could understand. But there's a bit more than that to this story. Not *much* more – but he'd have thought it a great deal. In your condition you might think so too. And I didn't want to risk upsetting you.'

Stephen worried when he heard that.

'Well you *have* upset me now,' he said.

The driver gave a rueful shake of his head.

'You'd think I'd know better,' he said. 'You may have forgotten who you are, but you're still the very same.'

Again the two men exchanged glances. But both of them were smiling now, amused. Stephen felt their amusement was at his expense, and he didn't like it one bit.

'Are you going to share the big joke or not?' he demanded.

'You may as well tell him,' the younger man said. 'Otherwise we'll have this all the way back.'

'Right,' Stephen said. 'I woke up two days ago knowing that I was a human, that I was a boy and that my name was Stephen – three simple things. Now I know I'm not human, and I'll be very surprised if my name's Stephen, and– '

'And you're not a boy,' the driver finished in a conversational tone. He caught sight of Stephen in the rear-view mirror, and he grinned. Stephen's face had gone blank. His mouth hung open.

'I ...' he began. 'You ...'

He turned to Kirsten, who was staring at him with a face almost as shocked as his own.

'I'm a *girl?*'

'Not exactly.'

'Stop talking in riddles!' A terrible thought struck him. A sick feeling grew in his stomach. 'Are you telling me,' he said, suddenly frantic, 'that I'm one of your ... *creatures?* Some kind of ... *tape-recorder?*'

'Lord no,' the driver said. 'But we're not human, don't forget. It's ... it's hard to explain to you. With humans – with most animal species nowadays – you have males and females, right?'

'Of course!'

'There's no "of course" about it. It's just an arrangement, like any other arrangement in nature. Plants can be male and female. Snails, now ... well that gets *very* complicated. But with the Sug and the Tellene, well ...'

He trailed off. Stephen was almost hopping in his seat with impatience.

'The old races were very different from each other,' the driver said. 'They had very different views of the world. Haven't you wondered how they managed to share a small island without murdering each other, good manners or not?'

'I thought they were ... you know ... *enlightened* or something.'

The driver snorted.

'*Enlightened!* They had a much more practical reason, child. They had only one gender apiece. They needed each other to continue their races.'

Stephen's mouth was sagging open again.

'They what?' he asked in a small voice.

'The Sug, do you see, were all male,' the driver said. 'Or as close to male as makes no difference. The Tellene were 'female'. I thought you might have guessed from my story – who else except men could spend ten thousand years *sulking*?'

Stephen was floundering badly now.

'But …' he said. 'But … the bodies ... ours … I mean …'

'Tut! Bodies are just things we make. Male bodies are simpler, easier to make, and males have things better among humans. So we generally come here as males, that's all.'

'But then why is Kirsten a girl?'

'Our children grow up here. As I told Simon, we want them to have memories. We want them to have memories appropriate to their actual nature. So they all grow as girls.'

'But then I …'

'You grew as a girl when you were first here.'

'*First?* But then I …' He looked suddenly blank again as he realised what the driver was getting at.

'How *old* am I?'

The driver considered. 'Oh, let's see. There was myself and my mother … that time in Babylon … hmmm.' He smiled at Stephen in the mirror. 'Roughly speaking, I'd say you're about three thousand years old. Give or take two hundred years.'

'And *who* am I? I thought I must be Kirsten's brother. Am I her *sister?*'

Again the two men laughed. Again the driver shook his head from side to side.

'We Tellene do believe in keeping business in the family,' he said. 'But Kirsten has only one sister.'

He nodded at the younger man beside him.

'*This* is Kirsten's sister,' he said.

'So you're, what, her mother?'

'No, I'm her aunt. But we do like our children to grow up with a parent nearby. We think it's healthier.' Even as he spoke, the driver was slowing the car. He stopped it and turned around in his seat, facing Stephen squarely. 'I don't want you to worry,' he said. 'There's really no need. But I can see that this is a bit of a surprise to you.'

'A *bit* of a–' Stephen stopped. He noticed that the driver was trying very hard not to laugh. Maybe Kirsten was trying too, but in her case it wasn't working. She'd begun to titter as her mind leaped ahead to the conclusion of the driver's news.

'*You're* Kirsten's mother,' the driver said. 'My little sister.'

Stephen felt as though someone had put a spell on him, a freezing spell, as the Sug in the chapel had done to Philip, or as the driver had briefly done to Stephen himself in the court-yard. He sat there like a statue. Around him in the car the other three, looking at him, began to laugh helplessly. For a moment Stephen teetered on the edge of anger. And then, with a sort of mental shrug, he joined in the laughter. The driver restarted the car. Stephen sat back in his seat. Kirsten put her arm through his. When he looked at her she was smiling at him.

'Well, Mum,' Kirsten said, 'here we are again, I suppose.'

'I suppose,' Stephen agreed.

'I'm glad we're related,' Kirsten said. 'I've got to like you in the past few days.'

Stephen sighed.

'Oh well,' he said, 'you know what they say.'

'What?'

'A girl's best friend is her mother.'

Kirsten giggled again. So did he – or she – or it.

If it matters.

42. Ministerial Functions

The Irish Minister for Defence looked out the window at the summer night. The summer night looked back in at him. Both of them were silent, but the Minister's brain was busy. He was thinking about big purple bubbles and little fat women who could walk through walls. It wasn't often that he thought about such things. Until a few days ago, in fact, he'd never given any thought to either.

The Minister looked bleakly around the office. There on the wall were the pictures of himself with various world leaders, the old team photos of rugby teams he'd played on, the pictures of himself as a young politician. Some people like to surround themselves with photos of themselves, as though they might somehow forget what they looked like – as though they might look in a mirror one day and find a stranger looking back.

The Big Bubble, Reputation One, had frightened the Minister very much. But the little fat woman had frightened him much more. That is, if it had been a woman at all. If so, what kind of woman? The kind that could walk through walls and paralyse with a single touch. The kind who could claim to be responsible for the Big Bubble in all its impossibility. The kind who spoke, moreover, in terms of 'we', meaning there were more like her. How many – a hundred? A thousand? Was there a whole army of little fat women in pink cardigans inside the Bubble? It hardly mattered. One of her was more than terrifying enough: how was a simple Minister for Defence to defend against a creature like that?

At least the Minister wasn't alone. The other men in the conference room, including the representatives of the most powerful countries on earth, had been thinking the same thing. It had been written plainly on their faces – mortal terror is hard to disguise. Even General Tubb had been shaking when a few moments after the woman left, he'd regained the use of his limbs.

The Minister for Defence felt unreal. He ran a finger absentmindedly along the surface of his desk, feeling the hard reality of the mahogany, the stiff leather corners of the blotter. They felt real enough. Maybe it was just him: maybe *he* was unreal.

The conference delegates had sworn an oath to keep the little fat woman's visit secret. They'd tell their governments, of course, but such things couldn't be revealed to the public. If the woman had been telling the truth and the Bubble disappeared, then it would go down as perhaps the greatest mystery in recorded history. If it didn't … well, they'd cross that bridge when they came to it.

The Minister looked at his watch. It was 10.36pm. Many of the delegates were still underground. Some had gone back to their hotels and embassies. The Minister had come up to his

office at around six, which meant he'd been sitting here thinking for four and a half hours. In all that time he hadn't had a
single pleasant thought.

There was a knock on the door. The Minister straightened
his collar and tried to look ministerial. It was hard when you
hadn't shaved in three days.

'Come in!' he called.

The excited face of his deputy popped round the door.

'Paddy!' she said. 'We've had a call! From the northwest! It's
gone!'

The Minister squawked.

'The northwest is *gone*?'

His deputy shook her head.

'No – the Bubble. The Phenomenon. It's disappeared!'

'Dis … it …' The Minister shook his head, to clear it. 'How
do you mean?'

'The word is it simply … disappeared,' she said. She was
very excited. 'The report said that one second it was there, and
the next it wasn't. As if it had been … switched off – like a
light.'

The Minister drew a very deep breath, and sat there holding
it for a very long time.

'Tell the army to get in there!' he roared then. 'And call my
helicopter!'

The Deputy Minister nodded and left. The Minister didn't
know whether to laugh or to cry. His telephone purred before
he'd had time to decide. The Minister picked it up. It was his
secretary. She said the Minister for Tourism was on the line.

He'd heard a report that the Big Bubble had vanished. He wanted to know what he was supposed to say to the Tourist Board. They were complaining already.

The Minister for Defence found himself grinning almost crazily.

'Tell the Minister for Tourism,' he said, 'to drop dead. Tell him I said so. Officially.'

43. Revels End

In a chapel in a monastery in the northwest of the island of Ireland, late one summer night in the last year of a gruesome century, a tall bearded man in dark robes landed hard on a stone floor with a sharp curse. He sat looking around him, blinking, as though surprised by the place he found himself in. The chapel, he saw, was lit only by the soft light of candles on the stone altar just behind him. He was alone.

The tall man stood up and rubbed the butt of his spine absentmindedly. He shook his head, then walked thoughtfully out of the chapel.

He met no one in the corridor outside, but passing the open door of the abbey's communal television room he saw a sight that made him smile. A young monk was curled up on the low round table there. The bearded man went in to waken the young man and pack him off to his bed. Had he been sleepwalking, perhaps? But the younger man looked so peaceful, and smiled so broadly in his sleep, that the bearded monk thought better of it. Leave him be.

As he neared the door of the room where he and his fellow monks had their meals, the big man thought he heard soft movement inside. He looked in through the open door.

Another tall man stood inside the room. He too was robed. He wore a skullcap on his salt-and-pepper hair. He was standing with his arms crossed, his chin cupped in one hand. He was staring at the ground, and he looked puzzled.

'Paul?' asked the bearded man. There was some hesitation in his voice.

The other man, startled, looked up.

'Philip!' he said. He sounded relieved. 'You gave me a fright.'

'How about a last cup of tea for the night?' Philip asked.

'Why not?' Paul said. 'My throat is very dry.'

The two men walked companionably to the front hall and looked out into the courtyard beyond. Light flooded from the open doorway into the kitchen wing, but otherwise all was dark.

'Someone's working late,' Paul said.

Philip gave a little chuckle.

'Simon. He likes to get everything ready for breakfast, but he prefers to do it when no one's around. He doesn't want us to know he's concerned about us.'

The abbot allowed himself a small smile.

'He has a gruff exterior,' he said, 'but he's a good man.'

'I know,' Philip said. 'I respect him.'

The two men walked towards the light. The soles of their sandals crunched on the gravel. It was a beautiful still night. The stars hung in heaven like lamps. The call of a night bird from the trees around the nearby lake was perfectly audible. The abbot looked up at the sky as they walked.

'The air is lovely tonight,' he said.

'Mountain air,' Philip agreed. 'A tonic in itself.'

In the kitchen they found Brother Simon asleep at the table, his head in his arms. He was smiling.

'He must have nodded off,' Philip said quietly. 'We should wake him.'

'The spirit is willing,' the abbot said fondly, 'but the flesh is weak. Simon is old, Philip. It frightens me sometimes to think how old he is.'

But the sound of their voices had already disturbed the old man's sleep. He stood up abruptly, groggy but fierce, looking blindly at them for a moment before some sleeping vision faded from his mind. He said something muffled and gruff in German, his tone questioning, demanding something from some figure in his dream.

'Was ist es, Simon?' Paul asked gently. 'Was willst du?'

But the old man at the table just shook his head and rubbed his eyes with both hands. He stood blinking at them, pale-faced.

'My word!' he said. 'Paul? Was I asleep? I had a dream, but … it's gone now.'

He blinked some more.

'What time is it?' he asked.

'I don't know. But it's late. Close to midnight, I'd say.'

Simon frowned in thought, trying to recall his dream. But it had shattered like soft crystal fragments, drifting and fading from his mind.

For a long moment the three men looked at each other in

silence, all somehow aware of something odd. But even that awareness faded as they stood. Then, in that silence, they heard them – faint and distant, but growing quickly both closer and louder. They were somewhere on the mountain road outside, howling like the demons from some dead superstition, like some utterly alien thing invading the peace of the hills and the glens: sirens, by the dozen, by the score, by the hundred, as the transports of the army and the fire service and the police and the reporters and the television crews and the thrillseekers and the rest of the wide world converged on that one lonely spot in the ruptured calm of the mild summer night.